Gangsta Luv 2: 'Til Death Do Us Part
Yvette Jazmyne Hunter

© Copyright 2013

Yvette Jazmyne Hunter

Printed in the United States of America.

Contact Jazmyne:

Author_Jazmyne@yahoo.com

yjhunter21@yahoo.com

www.facebook.com/author.jazmyne

www.facebook.com/yvette.hunter.35

Cover Design: Dynastys CoverMe

Acknowledgements

My parents: Anthony & Linda Hunter.

You guys are my rocks. I love y'all so much!

My sister's: Jasmine, Yvonne, & Yasmine.

I have no other choice but to acknowledge these ladies, they have been rocking with me since day one. Laurenae, Raychelle, Brandi, Danette, Enija, Charnitra, & Tamika. I thank y'all for that. Hell, if it wasn't for you all, I don't think I would have ever dropped any of my titles I did. Still can't wait for the day we all link up.

Tammie Tanner, rocks!!

I may be missing some people. If so I do apologize if I have left anyone out; please blame it on my mind and not my heart.

Aye, I bet y'all hating asses thought I forgot about y'all⋯ LMAO! Nah, I didn't. I'm going to need for y'all hating asses to keep doing what y'all are good at doing. And that's hating. Y'all motivate me to keep reaching for success.

Hi haters I see you⋯.. LMAO!

Dedications:

This book is dedicated to my little sister: Yasmine, Nieces: A'nya, Donnesti, NaNa, Kate'lyn & Kay'lah. My goddaughter: Jaliyah. Everything I do it for you ladies and know that I love y'all asses to pieces.

This book is dedicated to my damn self. I earned the right to say that!

Gangsta Luv 2: 'Til Death Do Us Part

A Novel By:

Jazmyne

Kendra,

Thanks for all
the love and support.

Jaymyne
A.K.A.

Vette

Chapter One

Kash stood looking out of the bay window staring into his backyard watching as the love of his life run around playing with the twins. They were growing right before his eyes and he knew before long that they would soon be drifting off into the cruel world they lived in all by their lonesome.

Nae badly wanted to move back to her home town of Oakland California and Kash agreed hoping for a fresh start. Something they both needed, but he would soon found out that moving to California wasn't one of the best decisions for neither of them as they tried to escape the allure of the game and its drama. But it would only follow them causing more hell and more drama than before.

"Daddy, come on," a two year old Lanaya said as she tugged at the bottom of Kash jeans. He smiled as he bent down to pick her up. She giggled as he carried her back outside. Kash had her spoiled rotten. Whatever her little heart desired she got. Lanaya and Keikeo had more clothes than your average adult and would soon grow out of but that didn't stop Kash from spoiling his kids with the finest things in life.

Kash stepped outside holding his princess in his arms as he watched Nae continuously chase Keikeo around.

This was the happiest he had seen Nae in a long time and was glad he was here to witness it. He had been through a lot in the past two years and so had she. Kash loved Nae even more for standing by his side when he was lying on his death bed. Any other bitch would have walked away but she stuck it out while she was pregnant and all. Kash loved Nae but that just made the bond and love they shared that much stronger.

"I see you finally decided to join us," Nae said as she walked over to Kash pecking him on the lips. Lanaya grabbed Kash face and turned it away from Nae. Kash and Nae both laughed. Lanaya hated sharing her daddy even with her mother.

"My daddy," Lanaya said as she buried her face into his neck and wrapping her tiny arms tightly around him.

Nae rolled her eyes and sucked her teeth. "Get ya daughter," Nae spat as she walked off. "Babe, what you got planned for the night?" Nae asked.

"Why, what do you have planned?" Kash asked back as Lanaya wiggled her way from his arms.

"Kendra and I are linking up tonight. I haven't seen my bitch in a long time and we tryna catch up," Nae answered.

"Nae, since we've been living in Cali all ya ass been doin' is running the streets 'Catching up' with *old* friends," Kash said taking a seat on one of the lounge chairs provided for guest.

"What's the big deal?" Nae asked.

Kash sighed, how could he deny her anything? Especially after what he had took her thru. "You know what ma, go enjoy ya self. But I do wanna meet Kendra," he said.

Nae smiled as she walked over sitting on his lap, she wrapped her arms around his neck kissing his lips tenderly.

"Aww thanks, babe. You're gonna love, Kendra," Nae said.

"Hold up, ma," Kash said patting Nae on her ass to lift her off his lap. His phone was ringing. He didn't bother checking the caller ID.

"What up?" He answered.

"You already know what time it is," the female voice said. Kash could hear the smile in her voice. He just knew the bitch was enjoying the bullshit. But sooner or later it would be coming to an end.

"I can't," he said as he looked over his shoulder to make sure Nae was nowhere in ear sight. She laughed.

"Kash, we don't play by ya rules anymore. I run this game and you do as I say," she said into the phone. "I'm sure you don't want wifey to find out about our little secret," she finished.

"Fuck," Kash mumbled under his breath as he stepped back into his house.

"If I make it to you I make it to you. If not, oh well," he said into the phone.

"Kash, I see you still don't get it-"

"Bitch, you still don't get it," he gritted thru clenched teeth cutting her off. "The only reason you haven't attempted to say shit to Nae is because you are afraid of what she's capable of doin' to you," he said pissed off.

She laughed. "Oh please you're the only one who's *afraid* of her," she shot back. "Just be at my place. I'm sure you know where it is. After all you did pay for it," she said laughing before hanging up on Kash.

Kash kept his composure as best he could. He had been dealing with that bitch for the last year and was sick and tired of it all. He wanted nothing more than to be happy and live the rest of his days without any problems with Nae. But he realized that problems seem to always follow him. It didn't matter how hard he tried to avoid the problems they always seem to find him and turn his world upside down.

"Is everything alright with you?" Nae asked as she walked into the kitchen. Kash turned and smiled as he pulled Nae in.

"Yeah, mothafuckas playing on my phone," he lied smoothly.

Nae looked at him with a raised eye brow.

Before Nae could begin her questioning, Keikeo run in behind her wrapping his arms around her leg. "Mommy, juice," he said looking up at her. Nae picked him up walking him over to the fridge to get him a juice box.

"Mommy, I want one too," Lanaya said running into the kitchen.

"What I tell you about running in the house?" Nae asked looking at her. Lanaya stopped dead in her tracks. Nae grabbed a juice box for Lanaya and handed it to her before putting her attention back on Kash.

"Don't think we aren't gonna talk about you and ya phone," Nae said as she handed Keikeo his juice box.

"That's cool," he said as his cell rung again. He looked at

the caller ID and smiled. He hadn't talked to his nigga in a while.

"What up, bruh?" Kash said into the phone as he walked off. He winked at Nae and she rolled her eyes flipping him off. He smacked her on the ass mouthing the word "When?"

Nae looked out the door to see what her babies were doing before picking up her phone to call Cherry. She hadn't talked to her in a while and wanted to know what she had been up too.

"Auntie hi," Jewel said answering the phone.

"Hi," Nae laughed. "What are you doin'?"

"Auntie, when can I come play with, Lanaya?" Jewel asked. "I miss y'all," she said.

"Aww, I miss you too. Let me talk to your mommy so that we can set a date for you to come see us," Nae told her.

"Okay, hold on. Mommy, auntie Nae on the phone for you," Jewel said.

"What I tell you about answering my damn phone," Nae heard Cherry asked before she got on the phone. "Roll ya eyes at me again and see what happen," Cherry said finally saying hello.

"I see you're having the same issues, huh?" Nae laughed.

"Girl, Jewel little ass is something else," Cherry said as she cut her eyes at her baby girl.

"I miss you bitch. What you been up too?"

"Girl, tryna get this damn agency open has what little time I do have for myself. Other than that I'm just tryna enjoy life," Cherry answered. "What about you?"

"Just living and enjoying myself. Getting back in the swing of living in Cali. Loving every minute of it," Nae told her.

"Who you tellin' there's nothing like home," Cherry laughed.

"Bitch you sound happy," Nae said.

"I am. No more drama or bullshit. We can finally put all that drama shit behind us," Cherry said referring to her and Ques.

Their relationship wasn't perfect just like any other relationship they had their ups and downs but they were strong enough to withstand it all.

"I agree, which is why I'm gonna enjoy it for as long as I can. Because fuckin' with Kash there's always something waiting to tear us down around every corner. "When are you coming to see us?" Nae asked changing the subject.

They hadn't seen each other or their girls since their vacation a little over a year ago.

"Whenever, I don't mind taking a little vacation," Cherry said.

"Jewel is gonna be a little mad with auntie because this trip is for the ladies," Nae said. "We're leaving them with their damn daddies," she laughed.

"That's cool with me. How about next weekend?" Cherry asked.

"That will be fine. There's this big party next weekend and we gonna show up and show the fuck out!" Nae said with excitement dancing in her voice. Cherry laughed.

"Good because I haven't been to a club in a long while and I can't wait to shake my ass," Cherry said.

"The only way you're shaking ya ass is if you shaking ya ass for me," Nae hear Ques say in the back ground.

"Tell that nigga to shut his ass up," Nae laughed. "Ain't anybody talkin' to his ass anyways," she said.

Cherry told Ques what Nae had said.

"Nae, don't make me fly all the way to Cali just to fuck you up, ma," Ques joked.

"Nae, I'm booking my flight as we speak," Cherry said grabbing her laptop.

"Yay, we going to see auntie Nae, and Lanaya, and Keikeo," Jewel sung in the background. Cherry and Nae laughed.

"Nae, you wanna break the bad news to her?" Cherry asked. "Cause you are not about to make me look like the bad guy," Cherry said.

"Noooo, I don't wanna look like the bad guy either," Nae laughed. "I gotta go, tell Jewel and JJ auntie loves them," Nae said not giving Cherry any time to protest.

"Aww I feel so bad," Nae said looking at her phone. Nae texted the rest of her girls before heading back outside with her, babies.

*

"Damn, bruh you just now dialing my math?" Kash asked as he inhaled the smoke from his blunt.

"Nigga, I been on the grind. I told you when I touch down I was gonna be on the paper chase hard," Shyne said.

Kash had met Shyne when they both were doing time up in Sing Sing. They had become close. Kash had got out before him. They kept in contact thru letters up until Shyne was released a few years later.

"I ain't mad at you. It's been two years and the streets are callin' me," Kash said.

"You're more than welcome to join forces with me," Shyne said offering Kash a spot on his team.

"No thanks and you know I work for no one but myself. I gave that shit up. I'm tryna turn over a new leaf," laughed Kash.

"Nigga, good luck. You know the streets are always gonna be a part of you. It don't matter how hard you try leaving it alone. The bitch has a way of always pulling you back in. It's in ya blood to hustle," Shyne said. "The streets need more niggas like us. We are a dying breed," he finished.

Kash agreed with him about being a dying breed. "Nah, that bitch taught me a lesson all ready. The same bitch I treated like a queen was the same bitch that turned her back on me and almost cost me my life," Kash said. "I'm good," he finished.

"I hear you talkin', but check this shit out. It's a party next weekend," Shyne said. "I want you to come out and show a nigga some love. Come see how I'm living," he said.

"That shouldn't be a problem. It's about time Cali gets used to seeing me," laughed Kash.

"A'ight, nigga I got ya math and you got mine. Holla if you need anything," Shyne said.

"Be easy, bruh, one," Kash said disconnecting the call.

Kash laughed as he thought on one of the many conversations he and Shyne had while they were locked up. Shyne had assured him time and time again that when he touched down and got on his feet he would be doin' the same thing that had landed him in jail in the first place.... Selling drugs. Kash believed him because he had said the same thing but now the drug game and anything dealing with the streets were behind him. Kash rubbed his chest as he thought on the many bullets he had taken just a few years prior. That was more than enough to make him give the game up. He had almost lost out on the most important thing in life, watching his kids grown up.

"Daddy, mommy leaving," Lanaya said as she skipped into the family room.

"Where is mommy goin'?" He asked laughing. She shrugged his shoulders as he sat his baby girl on his lap.

Kash heard a horn beep, standing up he carried Lanaya to the front door to see who it was as he headed for the door. Nae rushed past him.

"Babe, I'll see you later," she said blowing a kiss his way.

"Hold the fuck up. Fuck you in a rush for and who that?" He asked opening the front door.

"I told you, daddy," Lanaya smiled.

"I see I gotta teach yo ass about not snitch early," Nae laughed. Lanaya rolled her eyes.

"Did you just roll ya eyes at me?" Nae asked walking over to Kash.

"Chill," he laughed. "Kash, her little ass is out of hand, already," Nae spat.

"I wonder where she gets that from." He asked looking at Nae. Nae rolled her eyes before turning to walk out the front door. "My point has been proven."

"Damn, a nigga don't get a goodbye or nothing?"

Nae pecked him on the lips and said bye before rushing out the door. Kash stood at the door as he watched Nae jump in the nice ride sitting in front of his home.

"Bye, mommy," Keikeo said now standing next to Kash as he waved to Nae. Nae waved back before getting into the car. Kash watched as they slowly pulled off before he closed the door and looked at his babies.

"It's just us now. What are we gonna do?" He asked as he picked Keikeo up.

Kash smiled as Keikeo laid his head on his shoulder and closed his eyes. "It's like that?" He asked as he looked over at Lanaya who was dosing off as well. "Y'all are cold for leaving daddy up all alone," Kash said as he begin to climb the stairs to lay them down.

*

"Bitch, fill me in. What have I been missing out on?" Nae said as her and Kendra drove thru the streets of Oakland.

This was her home; she missed it something awful and was happy she was back.

"There isn't much to tell," Kendra replied. "You already know. It's the same game just different players," she shrugged.

Kendra smiled when her phone started ringing. "Hello?" She answered.

"What up, what you getting into today?" The male voice asked.

"I'm chillin' with my girl. She just moved back in town and we tryna catch up on missed time," Kendra answered. "Why, what's up?"

"I was tryna chill with you," he said. "Fuck y'all got plans to do anyways?"

"We are on our way to get Pedi's and madi's and we hitting the club tonight," she answered.

"A'ight, be safe ma, if you need me call me," he said before disconnecting the call.

"Okay, due tell who has you showing all thirty twos," Nae said as soon as Kendra removed her phone from her ear.

"Oh that's just Shyne. A nigga I'm tryna get to know a little better," Kendra answered waving her hand in the air as if it was nothing.

"Well it has to be something the way he has you cheesing," laughed Nae. "And it looks as if y'all know each other rather well."

Kendra laughed. "He's cool but he's another nigga deep in the streets. Don't get me wrong since we've been kicking it for the last six months he's made sure he spends time with me. I just don't wanna get all wrapped up and boom something happens," she said.

"Ken, don't hold back because if something happens it's gonna happen. Don't lose out on love," Nae said.

"Who the fuck said anything about love?" Kendra asked. "Don't get me wrong if it gets there that's what's up but I'm just living life and having fun," she finished.

"Yeah okay, you are talkin' all that shit now. You'll be singing a different tune soon," Nae assured. "Trust me I know."

"So, when am I goin' to meet Mr. Fiancé himself?" Kendra asked referring to Kash.

"Soon," Nae answered as she looked down at her purple diamond engagement ring Kash had place on her finger when he had waken from his coma.

Chapter Two

Cherry rushed around her room packing the rest of her things for her trip to Cali.

"Mommy, I'm all packed and ready to go," Jewel said as she skipped into the room holding her little purse tightly in her hands.

"Nae is wrong as hell for this," Cherry mumbled as she helped Jewel onto her king size bed. "Jewel, you aren't goin' with me to see auntie this trip," Cherry finally told her.

"But Auntie Nae said she was going to talk to you. I wanna go see Lanaya, Keikeo, and uncle Kash," Jewel pouted as she looked at Cherry with her big brown puppy dog eyes.

"I know and I promise you next time you can go," Cherry said.

"Mommy, I wanna go," Jewel continued to pout. "I'm going to call auntie," she said climbing off the bed with the help of Cherry. Who was laughing, as she watched Jewel run out of her bedroom.

"Whoa, slow down lil ma," Jacques said as he stepped to the side as Jewel zoomed past him. "What up babe fuck you goin'?" He asked seeing Cherry open suitcases sitting across the bed.

"Ques, don't act like you don't know. I've been tellin' you for the past few days that I'm goin' to Cali to see Nae and the rest of my girls," Cherry answered as she resumed packing.

"You need all that for a few days?" He asked removing his shirt.

"A lady can never have enough clothes," Cherry answered rolling her eyes.

"So you just gonna up and leave me with the kids?"

"Ques, they are your fuckin' kids too," Cherry said becoming annoyed.

"Damn, what's with the attitude? I was only playing," he said.

"Whatever," Cherry replied as she finished packing her things.

"How long are you gonna be gone again?" He asked.

"I'm goin' to be gone five days the most, why?" Cherry asked.

"Just asked," Ques answered already with his mind made up that him and his niggas were crashing whatever plans Cherry and her girls had.

"Ques, whatever you have planned please dead that shit," Cherry said.

"Ma, fuck you talkin' about? My babies and I are just gonna chill while you're away," Jacques lied.

"Have fun because I know I will," Cherry said handing him one of her bags.

Jacques looked from his hand to Cherry. "So you just

gonna leave a nigga hanging? No goodbye loving or nothing?" He asked.

"Playa you knew you wanted some last night. I got a plane to catch," Cherry said trying to hide her smile.

"Ma, that's fucked up and you know it," Jacques said pissed.

"I got you when I get back home," she promised as she left the room.

Jacques followed closely behind her mumbling some shit she couldn't understand.

"JJ and Jewel come give me a hug," Cherry said sitting her bags by the door. JJ paused the game he was playing before jumping up and running to Cherry.

"Bye, mommy," he said as he ran into her arms wrapping his arms around her.

Jewel slowly walked to Cherry holding her phone in her hand. "Auntie didn't answer," she said giving Cherry a hug.

"As soon as I see her I'm gonna tell her to call you," Cherry promised.

"Okay," Jewel said turning and running off to play.

"Are you sure you don't want me to drive you to the airport?" Jacques asked. Cherry shook her head no.

"I'll call you when I get there. Have fun, bye," She said hearing a horn beeping. She grabbed her bag and Jacques grabbed the other helping her to the awaiting cab.

Jacques placed Cherry bags in the trunk before closing the

door.

"Ma, be safe out there and don't make me have to come to Cali to fuck one of them west coast niggas up," he said as Cherry slipped into the back of the cab.

Cherry laughed. "I plan to have fun but I can't control what niggas think of me," she said closing the door.

"Be easy," he said leaning in thru the window to give his lady a kiss. He tapped the top of the cab to let the driver know that it was now safe to pull off.

Jacques stood and watched as the cab eased out of their drive way. He turned to find JJ waving bye.

"Lil' man, it looks like it's just us three. What you wanna do?" He asked as they went back into the house and closed the door behind them.

JJ pointed to the video game before walking off. Jewel sat in the middle of the room playing with a few of her baby dolls.

Jacques knew he had come a long way from the hustling nigga he was. A few years ago he didn't give a fuck about much. He was chasing paper and that's all that matter, until he met Cherry. She had taught him the sex wasn't better than love. Since they had met it had always been a tear for a tear and eye for eye. But Jacques knew that Cherry wasn't just his love she was also his homey. Jacques knew he had taken Cherry or a ride most bitches couldn't handle and would have asked to get off of a long time ago. She hung in there and thugged it out. *"That's my baby."* He thought.

His cell phone rang.

"Speak on it," he answered.

"This nigga done moved to the A and forgot all about his niggas," Melo said. Jacques sucked his teeth.

"Fuck outta here. Y'all niggas got my math too," he spat. "I thought Ray killed ya weak ass already," he laughed. Chase, King, Kash, and Melo all laughed.

"Fuck outta here. You know my baby don't fuck with weak niggas," Melo said. "You already know I'm a built to last kind of nigga." He said.

"What's really good with y'all niggas?" King asked.

"Word, it's about that time we link up. It's been a minute," Chase said.

"Is it okay for y'all niggas to do anything?" Kash laughed.

"Fuck you!" Melo laughed too. "Ray ass on her way to you," he informed Kash.

Kash fucked with Nae girls but having them all together in one room was too much. They were wild as fuck. He loved them but he couldn't handle them all by his lone self.

"WHAT? Fuck you mean?" Kash asked. "Why the fuck y'all niggas just tellin' me this?"

"You know they asses stay having conference calls. They were planning a ladies weekend with Nae this weekend," Chase laughed.

"The fuck? Aww hell no," Kash said. "I'm not with it."

"You better get with it because they should be showing up at any time," King said.

"Fuck it we might as well make it a family reunion," Chase said.

"That's what it's goin' to be, because there's no way in hell I'm dealing with all them by myself," Kash said.

"Say no more. I'm jumping on the next flight. Jewel lil' ass been trying her hardest to get to you anyways," Jacques said.

"Bring my niece. Lanaya has been asking for her too," Kash said.

"We'll see you in a few hours," Chase said.

"One," They all said at the same time before hanging up.

"Jewel, guess what, momma?" Jacques said looking over at his daughter.

She looked up at him batting her eyelashes.

"We're goin' to Cali to see uncle Kash after all.

"YAY!" She said as she jumped to her feet.

*

Cherry sat in the back seat of the taxi lost in her thoughts. The last two years had been crazy for her and Jacques and she was glad that it was finally over. They had weathered the storm. Cherry knew there was no such thing as living happily ever after. Around every corner was more bullshit and drama waiting to tear them apart. They had proven that their love was strong enough to withstand anything.

She just hoped and prayed that Atlanta welcomed them with open arms. Since they've been living there they hadn't ran across any bullshit but Cherry sensed that some type of trouble was on the horizon. Trouble seems to always invite itself where it didn't belong or wasn't wanted.

A small smile spread across her lips as she thought on the day she killed G. It was one of the easiest kills she had done. The nigga would have done anything just to get a taste of her pussy. Cherry shook her head as she thought of, One. Now he was the one she wanted to personally put a bullet between his eyes but her girl Ray had taken him out right on the court room stairs. The same day he was supposed to testify against Jacques. She did take pleasure in watching his head explode like a melon.

Living the fast life wasn't appealing anymore. She had been there and done that. All she wanted to do now was watch her babies grow up while she prayed and hoped when they grew up they took a different route. But who was she kidding? Hustling was in their blood. At one point in time Cherry loved everything about the game. From the lavish life it offered to the unexpected events it held. She use to get a big rush when she held any gun of her choice to any of her victims faces. The fear they showed and the power she felt rushed thru her veins was like a high she could never get back. But that was when she was young and wild. She had grown up and had a different outlook on life, now that she had kids of her own.

Did Cherry regret any of the things she had done in her past? No, it was taken as a lesson learned.

Cherry looked up to find the cabdriver staring at her breast thru the rearview mirror.

"See something you like?" She smiled leaning forward in her seat to give him a better view. He licked his lips.

"Ma'am, are those real?" He had the nerve to ask.

"Ask my man. He knows," Cherry spat. "You perverted bastard," she said leaning back in her seat. "You better keep ya eyes where they belong and that's on the road ahead of you." She told him. "Before you are missing 'em," she finished.

"You are a feisty one," he smiled showing off his nasty mouth.

"Baby, you just don't know how feisty I am," Cherry said. "And you really don't wanna find out," she warned with a roll of her eyes.

Cherry searched her purse for her ringing cell phone. "Hello?" She answered.

"BITCH!" Vonne said. Cherry laughed.

"Hey," she replied.

"Hey, is all a bitch gets? Fuck you been up too? I haven't talk to ya ass since you and Ques punk ass moved to Atlanta," Vonne said.

"I just have been real busy trying to get the modeling agency open," Cherry answered. "And let's not forget raising two spoiled bad ass kids," she laughed.

"What up with my god babies?" Vonne laughed.

"You need to come get ya bad ass god babies," Cherry

said.

"I love 'em but you know I don't do well with kids. For some strange reason me and kids just don't mix," she laughed.

"You are goin' to Cali too right?" Cherry asked.

"I live in Cali, have you forgotten?" Vonne asked. "Anyho, what's really good? I haven't seen any of my bitches in forever and a day. I'm tryna link up and get shit poppin' like old times," she finished.

"Well Nae has invited all of us out to Cali for a ladies weekend. I thought you knew?"

"Oh so Nae just said fuck Vonne. I see how she does," Vonne said faking hurt.

"Bitch, if you stay off ya phone long enough to get a phone call you would have known," Cherry said.

It didn't matter what Vonne was doing or where she was, her phone stayed glued to her ear. Her ass stayed caking.

"You ain't gonna believe me but I just got my phone back. I dropped it in water and the shit stopped working. I was sick without my baby," Vonne laughed.

"Why am I not surprised?" Cherry said shaking her head. "I'll text you her address and we should be seeing you there, right?"

"Hell yeah I'll be there," Vonne said.

"A'ight, I'll see you there," Cherry said hanging up.

"Is ya girls as pretty as you?" The cab driver asked once

again eyeing Cherry thru the rearview mirror. Cherry rolled her eyes as she text Vonne Nae address.

"That's something you will never find out," Cherry said as she placed her phone back in her purse. "Please stop talkin' to me and do ya job. Which is driving me to my destination?"

"I'm just trying to spark a conversation with a pretty lady," he said.

"No need, there isn't anything we have to talk about," Cherry said as she reached into her purse for her IPod. She placed her ear buds in her ear and hit play tuning the cabbie and anything else he had to say out. She couldn't get to the airport fast enough.

During the entire ride, Cherry would catch him staring at her thru the rearview mirror. She ignored it, because she knew she wouldn't be in his presences to much longer.

Chapter Three

"Nae," Kash called walking thru the house.

"What?" She asked standing in the kitchen.

"When was you gonna tell me you invited ya girls out here?" He asked now standing at the island.

"I didn't know I had to tell you that," Nae said.

"How you know I wanna be around they asses all weekend?" He asked. "What, is this one of ya men bashing things?" He asked. Nae rolled her eyes.

"No, this is about us. We haven't seen each other since our last vacation and I wanted to chill with my bitches," she let him know. "And you can take ya ass somewhere if you don't wanna be here," she said.

"Why I gotta get penciled in to spend time with you?" Kash asked totally ignoring her last statement.

"You don't. Why are you tripping?" She asked.

"I'm not trippin' yet. You know what have fun, fuck it I'm up," he said chucking up the deuces as he left the kitchen.

"He's not about to fuck up my day," Nae mumbled.

As of lately Kash seem to be on the edge all the time. Nae noticed it but didn't know why. At first she chucked it up as him living in a new place. Kash was New York to the day he died and living in Cali would take some time in getting use too. But they had been living in Cali for over a year now. She knew he was used to it by now. It was something else; she knew it and would soon found out just what had him on the edge. She just prayed it wasn't bullshit. Who was she kidding bullshit was always waiting for them. "Whatever," Nae said. She didn't have time for Kash or his so called attitude.

"Mommy, the door," Keikeo said as he ran into the kitchen with his sister hot on his heels.

"What I tell y'all asses about running in the house?" She asked. They stopped running but it was too late they were already in trouble.

"Where's my daddy?" Lanaya asked.

"Girl, bye he isn't gonna save you. Let me have to tell y'all about running in my house again," Nae said. "I'm gonna spank both y'all hardheaded asses," she warned.

Lanaya rolled her eyes as she walked the other way. Keikeo followed Nae to the door.

Nae opened the door to find Ray standing there. "HEY!" Nae sung as they shared a hug.

"Bitch, why I had to curse the cab driver out," Ray said as she stepped inside.

"Hi Auntie Ray," Keikeo said as he hid behind Nae.

"Sup, lil' man?" She asked as she grabbing and picked him up. "Give me a hug," she said. He wrapped his arm around her neck.

"Damn, Keikeo got big," Ray said as she put him down.

"Tell me about it," Nae laughed as they walked into the kitchen. "When are you and Melo gonna give me a niece or nephew?"

"Melo ass is playing. I'm tryna pop one out ASAP," Ray said taking a seat at the island.

Nae got Ray a glass and a bottle of Ciroc. "Bitch, I'll take that but where is the Cali loud. I need that in my life," Ray said. "The party is finally here. Oh and before I forget, I got my stripper friends on call just in case we need 'em," she laughed.

"Call they asses, I got a few dollars I wanna spend," Nae joked on her way to answer the door once again. She thought it was Kendra.

She opened the door and laughed. "Oh no, bitch don't laugh. How you gonna have a ladies weekend without me?" She asked walking right pass Nae. "Damn, this shit nice," she said looking around.

"First off bitch, I called you at least ten times and left you message after message," Nae said rolling her eyes. "You never answered or called me back."

"My bad but I just got my phone back. I dropped it in some water and them mothafuckas gonna take forever and a day to send me a new one," Vonne said as Nae showed her the way to the kitchen.

"Vonne!" Ray said.

"Ray, what's really good?" Vonne asked as they hugged.

"Ain't shit, tryna get my party on. Waiting for Nae stingy ass to pull out the Cali loud," Ray joked.

"Aye, I'm right on time," Vonne said talking a seat.

"Hi, Auntie Ray and Vonne," Lanaya said skipping into the kitchen.

"Oh god. Nae look at her. She's too cute," Vonne said. "Girl, you are almost as cute as me."

Vonne had Nae and Ray rolling. "Give me a hug," Vonne said getting off the stool. Lanaya rolled her eyes before she turned and walked off. "Girl, is something wrong with her eyes?" Nae you know I fight kids," Vonne said sitting back down.

"That little girl is a trip," Nae said.

"Where that nigga, Kash at?" Ray asked.

"Hell if I know. That nigga stormed out talkin' bout he didn't wanna be around me and my girls all weekend."

"Eww, nobody wants to be around his whack ass," Vonne said pouring her a drink.

"I see I'm a have to put my paws on his ass one good time," Ray said.

Vonne spit out her juice as she burst out laughing. Nae was weak.

They kicked it while they waited for the rest of their girls to show up.

*

Kash rode thru the streets of Oakland Cali. This was very unfamiliar territory but he had mastered most of what he needed to know. Being that Cali would be his home for the long run. They city was nice but Kash felt that there will never be nothing like home. New York had a way of pulling and sucking you in. He would soon find out, Cali was the same way. Kash had been stressing for the longest and it wasn't gonna ease up anytime soon. He had Nae on one hand and this bitch on the other demanding all his time and attention. *"I should have been bodied this bitch."* He thought.

Kash kept telling himself that he was doing what he had to do to protect Nae but in all reality he wasn't. He was digging himself into a deep hole; he soon would need help getting out of.

"Fuck! I can't lose my baby," he mumbled running his hand thru his waves. Kash knew he had to end things. "How in the hell am I gonna tell my baby about this without losing her?" He asked himself.

Kash pulled up to his destination, sitting in the car for a while longer. His mind was already made up but he knew how much of a bitch she was. She was gonna make his life even more complicated. "This is the life of being that nigga," he chuckled climbing out of his car.

Before he could knock on the front door, the door flew open.

"So it takes you a whole fuckin' week to get over here?" She asked with her hands on her hips.

"Bitch move," Kash said as he brushed passed her. "You better be happy a nigga showed up." He said looking around the place as if he hadn't been there before.

"Kamil-"

"Hold up. You don't have any right callin' me by my government name. So refrain from using it," he said cutting her off.

"I see you still don't get it. Kash as of now I got ya black ass by the balls," she smirked. "What I say goes. With that being said bring ya fine ass over here and fuck this pussy. We missed you," she purred as she sat on her leather sofa with her legs spread eagle showing her shaved pussy.

Kash wasn't turned on at all. "I see you still don't get it. Bitch, you don't have me by shit. I've played ya game long enough and as of today it has come to an end," he assured. "What you fail to realize is that Nae has my heart and always will. You or the next bitch can't change that." He finished turning to walk away.

"Kash, walk out that door and I will make ya life a living hell," she said jumping to her feet. Kash laughed.

"Bitch, you can't make my life a living hell when I live in hell on a daily bases," he turned so that she could look in his face to see just how serious he was. "The only time my life seems to shine bring is when I'm with my lady and kids. You can try though, good luck." He finished leaving her standing there confused.

"No, this isn't happening!" She yelled as she found her plan crumbling right before her eyes. She knew just what Kash and Nae were capable of but at this point she had no other choice but to try her hand. She had one up on Nae and would be using it to her advantage. She knew Kash wouldn't tell her about them because of his fear of losing her.

"This bitch has got to go. She's in my way of happiness."

She thought as she grabbed the candle holder throwing it across the room.

"I have to get him back here and plead my case," she mumbled as she searched for her phone.

*

Shyne was deep in the streets but ever since he had met Kendra he used all his free time chasing her down. She had been the only chick in a long time to grab his attention. It didn't matter what he did she stayed occupying his mind. But as of lately he has only seen her here and there. Something he wasn't feeling. He wanted to know what was up with the sudden change.

Kendra was definitely different. She wasn't pleased with how much money he had or his big houses nor was she pleased by the fly whips he drove. For every stack he pulled out she pulled out two more, for every house he had showed her, she had shown him one better, and for every nice whip he sported she showed that she too had one. How could he not fall for her?

Shyne hadn't found a female who talked her mind and didn't sugar coat shit. When she didn't like something she let it be known. Not to mention she could cook her ass off. Everybody knows a way to a nigga's heart is through his stomach. Not to mention her beauty. She was definitely one to take home to his momma.

Shyne walked thru the mall looking for an outfit for the party he was throwing tomorrow night. He removed his phone from his pocket about to dial Kendra's number but stopped when he spotted her caking with some nigga. Shyne placed his phone back in his pocket while he walked towards her.

"My man you good. She's already taken," Shyne said as he draped his arm around her shoulder looking dude in his face.

"My bad, Shyne, I didn't know she was ya girl," the guy said backing off.

"Well now you do," Shyne said mean mugging the dude until he was a good distances away.

"Excuse you," Kendra said removing his arm from around her. "Since when did I become ya girl?" She asked.

"Since the day we met. I told you I wanted you," he said. "I'm a boss nigga and it's only right I got a boss bitch right by my side."

Kendra laughed as she punched him in his chest. "Don't be doin' no shit like that," she said turning to walk off.

"Fuck you mean? I don't take well to other niggas all over what's mine," he said grabbing her arm. Shyne turned her around to face him again.

Kendra was feeling Shyne way more than she was showing. She knew how shit went when dealing with niggas like Shyne. She just didn't wanna end up with a broken heart.

Shyne was tall standing a good 6 foot 6 inches. Smooth butter pecan skin sexy bedroom brown eyes and a smile that made you fall in love with him, with long dreads that he kept held together in a ponytail. His body was just an added bonus. Kendra knew he took pride in taking care of his body. His swag was always on point and since they had met a few months back she was yet to see him rock the same thing twice.

"Just what I said, I see you tryna fuck up my game," she said.

"Ma, you mind as well end all that. Let those niggas know that daddy's home," Shyne said draping his arm around her pulling her close.

"Whatever," Kendra laughed as she rolled her eyes playfully. "Where ya hoes at?" She asked looking around.

"I don't have hoes. I'm single but I'm tryna give that title up only if you fuck with a nigga though," he whispered in her ear.

"I'm sure you tell all those bitches that," Kendra said.

"Trust me I don't. I only look for one night stands with hoes and they know that," he said. "I don't wife hoes because I don't love those hoes," he laughed.

"Shut up," Kendra laughed. "What you getting into?"

"Hopefully you one day," he answered smacking her on her ass. The skinny leg jeans she had on had her ass looking fatter than usual. The way they hugged the lower part of her body had him wishing he could switch positions with 'em just for a second.

"Stop playing," she said pushing him away.

"My bad ma. I couldn't help it. Them jeans you got on got a nigga mind wondering a lot," he smiled show casing his sexy smile. "Anyhow a nigga hungry. What about you?"

"I guess I can spend some time with you before I go kick it with my girl," Kendra said.

"Oh baby you didn't have a choice," Shyne said wrapping both arms around her as they walked thru the mall laughing and joking with each other.

*

Kash felt as if his life was spinning out of control. It didn't matter how hard he tried to grip it, it always slipped thru the open spaces. He just hoped Nae understood while he prayed they made it thru this situation just as they did the others. Kash knew this one was way different. He had crossed the line when he slept with her, brought her that condo and paid for her plastic surgery. When Nae got wind of all that, he knew for a fact life as he knew it was over.

"Why the fuck can't a nigga just be happy?" He asked himself. "It's as if Nae and I don't belong together."

Kash needed to wrap his mind around everything and prepare himself for the storm that was on its way. If anybody thought New York was bad, they hadn't seen anything yet. He just hoped they weathered this storm as well.

*

When Kash stepped into his home he could hear laughter coming from the kitchen. He knew that Nae girls had arrived and he was just in time for the festivities.

He slowly walked into the kitchen to find bottles of liquor and food all over the place.

"I see the party started without me," he said letting it be

known he was there.

They all continued their conversation as if he hadn't just said anything. "Well hello to y'all too," he said a little louder.

"Poof be gone, nigga," Ray said as she waved her hand in the air. Her girls laughed.

"Ray, you gone leave my baby alone," Nae said.

"What up nigga, long time no see, huh?" Cherry asked as she walked over to him to give him a hug.

"Not long enough," he laughed. She punched him in his chest.

"Damn girl," he said rubbing his chest. Kash looked around the kitchen and smiled. Seeing Nae and her girls brought back old memories good ones at that.

"I see some shit will never change," he said walking over to Ray snatching the blunt from her hand.

"Come on nigga, all these blunts in rotation you take mine?" She asked. Kash went to hug her but she pushed him away. "Now you know I don't do that lovey dovey shit," she said taking her blunt back.

"Aye, Ray what up you gonna call some of ya stripper friends up or what?" Dani asked.

"Word, I'm tryna see a nigga twerk something for these one's I got in my purse," Brandi laughed.

"Y'all better call them niggas somewhere else. The only nigga shaking anything for Nae is me," Kash said as he grabbed the bottle of Hennessy. "Isn't that right, ma?" He asked smacking Nae on her ass.

"Not this weekend," Nae laughed high as hell.

"Nae don't play with me," Kash warned.

"She ain't playing. Nigga, we didn't come to Cali just to stare at you all day," Vonne said. "If I wanted to look at you all day I would have pulled out an old pic."

"Kash, you gotta go. You fuckin' our groove up," Nija finally spoke.

"Iight, I'm about to go chill with my babies," Kash said. Before he left the kitchen he grabbed Nae. "I love you girl," he said kissing her lips.

"I love you too," she replied kissing him back.

"Come on now I'm tryna keep the food I just ate down," Ray said holding her hand over her mouth. Both Nae and Kash flipped her off as everyone else laughed.

Kash smiled because he knew they were gonna all be pissed when his niggas showed up. *"How they gonna party without the whole crew?"* He thought as he was in search of his babies.

Day had turned into night as the partying continued. Kash niggas had finally showed up, pissing the ladies off.

"Kash really?" Nae asked.

"What?" He asked.

"Why you invite ya niggas knowing I was having a ladies weekend with my girls?" She asked standing in the kid's door way as she watched Kash lay Janaya and Jewel down before he tucked them in.

"What that gotta do with my niggas being in town?" He asked.

"You're a jackass for that. I got you," she warned before walking off.

Kash checked on JJ and Keikeo before he turned the lights out closing the door behind him making his way to his niggas.

*

Kash walked in the fully furnished basement to find Melo and Chase in a heated argument about the basketball game they were playing on the PlayStation 3.

Kash laughed as he fixed himself a drink. He looked at the cup and the bottle of Hennessy before grabbing the bottle leaving the cup he had just poured sitting on the counter. He made his way over to the pool table when Jacques and King were in the middle of a heated game as well. Money was on the line for both games that were taking place, nobody wanted to lose but there was always a loser at the end of every game that was played.

"What's really good with you niggas?" Kash asked taking a seat and a swig from the bottle.

It took a minute for anyone to respond as everyone was tryna stay focus on the task at hand.

"This past year has been one of the best years of my life," Jacques answered. "But you know living happily ever after only happens in those damn urban books Cherry collects," he said.

"Why you say that?" King asked standing off to the side.

"Because it's as if my past won't leave me the fuck alone," Jacques said.

"Tuh, I guess I'm not the only one having issues, huh?" Kash asked taking another swig from the bottle.

"The past won't stay where it belongs. In the fuckin' past," Ques answered.

"Fill us in," Melo said pausing the game.

"For starters I got this one stalker bitch that won't leave me alone-"

"Who?" Chase asked cutting him off.

"Y'all remember Anna, right?"

"Anna?" They all asked at once.

Anna was a bitch Jacques use to fuck with way back in the day. She had been obsessed with him for years. She had disappeared years ago, no one had heard or seen her since.

"Fuck she came from?" Kash asked.

"Bruh, I don't know nor do I give a fuck. I just wish the bitch would have stayed under the rock she crawled from," Jacques said walking to the counter grabbing the cup of Hennessy Kash had poured. He took the cup to the head before sitting the empty cup back on the counter. He patted his chest from the burning sensation the Hennessy had caused.

"How she get ya math, bruh?" King asked lighting a blunt. Jacques shrugged his shoulders.

"Nigga, you know shit real. When I was leaving to catch my flight the bitch was standing at my front door. I damn near dropped dead," Jacques said causing his niggas to laugh. "Man, this shit ain't even funny. Shit, I can only imagine what Cherry would do if she finds out," he sighed running his hands thru his dreads.

"Oh damn. Yeah, bruh you better handle that," Melo said.

"I tried, the bitch gone tell me if she can't have me no one can," Jacques said.

"I'll go cop my black suit tomorrow," Chase said.

Brandi and her girls didn't play that shit. They were no nonsense type of chicks. That cheating and having other bitches on the side wasn't accepted. But who would cheat on chicks like them anyways? They were one of a kind type of ladies. The type of ladies you would love to bring home to ya mother. One's who had ya back no matter what.

"You better get rid of ole girl or tell Cherry. That's how you almost lost her the last time," King said. "Keeping things like that from her." He finished.

Kash blurted out something. "What?" They all asked looking at him. It wasn't that they didn't hear him. They all wanted to make sure they had heard him right. Kash repeated what he had said.

"Aww, hell no!" Chase said.

"Bruh, what the fuck was you thinking?" King asked.

"You should have bodied that bitch when she first approached you," Melo spat.

"The question is what the fuck do you wanna be buried in?" Jacques asked. "Nae, definitely gonna kill you, son."

"He wasn't thinking," King said.

"The fuck was I supposed to do?" Kash asked jumping to his feet.

"Pipe down, homey. We ain't the ones to take ya anger out on," Melo spat.

"You were supposed to take that bitch out the day she stepped to you," Chase answered.

"She's blackmailing me," Kash said.

"A dead bitch can't blackmail anyone," Jacques assured.

"I fucked up," Kash said.

"DUH!" They all sung. Kash waved them all off as he left the basement. He needed to be alone to get his mind right. He grabbed a few of the blunts already rolled before walking out.

Kash walked thru his home. He didn't hear anything and knew that the ladies had gone out. *"Good."* He thought as he made he was to the back door. He opened the door stepping out closing the door behind him.

The night air felt good brushing up against his face sobering him up a little. He stood staring out into space.

All he really wanted to do was keep Nae happy. Kash had never been in love like he was with Nae. She completed him on every level, but he couldn't seem to get rid of bullshit. Just about all the good and bad memories they shared, Kash could say he had only been thru what he been thru with Nae. Kash lowered his head sighing deeply as he remembered what Nae had said.

"Kamil, all I'm lookin' for is love because I already have everything else. All I need is for someone to mean what they say when they say they love me," Nae said. "And that's gonna hold me when I need to be held. Someone who knows when my day didn't go well and tell me that tomorrow will be better."

Over the years Kash tried to fulfill her wish every day. He loved to see her smile, he loved everything about her. He never wanted to hurt her but he knew once the cat was out of the bag, things between them would forever be different.

"Are you okay?" King asked as he stepped outside.

"How can I be fine? When I stepped out on my wife for selfish reasons?" Kash asked. "At the time I thought I didn't have a choice but I did. I just choose to do the wrong thing."

"Bruh, everybody makes mistakes, as long as you work on fixing them and making things right," King said.

"King, the one woman I find that only asked me to love and protect her and I can't even do that right," Kash spat running his hands over his waves.

"Listen, you can't change what's done. The only thing you can do now is move on and work on making it right again," King said. "The love you and Nae share is rare. This may tear y'all apart for a moment that's about it, neither of you can deny the love y'all have for each other."

"Sometimes I feel like just letting go, not because I don't love her but because I don't wanna keep hurting her," Kash said.

"So stop hurting her and love her like you promised to do," King said.

"King, it's like no one wants to see us happy. If it isn't one thing it's another," Kash said.

"Kash, fuck what everyone else thinks or how they feel about you and Nae. The only person you should care about thinking anything is, Nae," King spat. "This should be all the more reason to show mothafuckas that the bond you two share is unbreakable."

"Man, I don't know-"

"You don't know what?" King asked. "I dare you say some stupid shit. I'm gonna punch that shit right back in ya mouth," he warned.

Kash looked at his little brother and knew he was serious.

"Kash, you and Nae have already been tested time and time again only to come out on top. This is just another test to see how strong y'all are. Remember relationships aren't perfect. But when it's all said and done make sure she doesn't have enough hands to use to count all the good things you've done for her and only one hand for all the bad or hurt you have ever caused her," King said before walking back inside the house, leaving Kash with something to think about.

Chapter Four

Kash sat in the basement listening to Hood Love by Mary and Trey Songz deep in his thoughts. It had been a week since his boys has left and went back home. He was stressing more than ever. The only good thing about everything was that nothing had happened. He knew he had to tell Nae, he just didn't know how. As of lately he had been walking around on edge. The only things that seem to ease his racing mind was when he was spending time with his kids and Nae. That's when she and Kendra weren't running around all crazy. Kash laughed because Kendra fit right in with Nae and her girls. She was just as crazy as the rest of them.

"There you are," Nae said as she walked into the basement. "Are you okay?" She asked.

"I'm good," replied Kash as he looked up at her to find her dressed in a pair of black skinny leg jeans and tank top.

"Where are you goin' now?" He asked.

"Nowhere, Kendra is on her way to pick up the kids so that you and I can spend some time together," Nae answered sitting on his lap.

"Word? That's nice," Kash said.

"Kash, what's up with you?" Nae asked sensing something was bothering him.

"Nothing is up with me."

"It has to be something. Since we've moved to Cali, you

haven't been yourself, why?"

"Fuck!" Kash thought as he laid his head back closing his eyes. He knew this was his chance to tell Nae what was going on but he couldn't bring himself to do it.

"Why are you lying to me?" She asked.

"Fuck it. I rather tell her the truth than hurt her with a lie." Kash thought. "Nae, I been fuckin' with Maria-"

"WHAT?!" She asked slapping the shit out of him. "You have been fuckin' who?" She asked now standing over him.

"Chill the fuck out!" Kash barked jumping to his feet.

"So that bitch is the reason you've been walking around acting all funny?" Nae asked holding back the tears.

"I can explain-"

"Fuck you nigga. You don't have to explain shit. I'm up," she spat as she stormed out. She stopped in her tracks turning to face Kash once again. "You fucked that bitch didn't you?" She asked. Kash lowered his head answering her question.

"Out of all the bitches you could have picked to fuck you pick her?" Nae asked shaking her head. Nae looked down at her engagement ring and couldn't stop the tears from falling. "I hope she was worth it." She said finally leaving the room.

"I can explain," Kash said chasing after her.

"Fuck you! And save ya lame ass excuses," Nae said as she

jerked herself from his grip. "How could you?" She asked looking at him.

"I had no choice," Kash answered. Nae laughed.

"You have no choice to fuck another bitch?" She asked in disbelief. "Well since you didn't have a choice you got one now," she said turning to walk away. Kash went to grab her. "Don't you dear fuckin' touch me!" She yelled.

"Nae, we need to talk about this," Kash said watching her walk away. Nae flipped him two birds as she went to get her babies from the playroom.

Kash ran after her. "She's black mailing me. I did this for you, for us," Kash said grabbing her to face him. Nae laughed.

"So, you fucked the next bitch for me, for us?" She asked. "That's the first time I've heard that before. Kash I'm done you can continuing fuck that bitch, for you," she finished as she picked up her babies one by one.

"Nae, I understand if you need a break but you aren't taking my kids anywhere," Kash said as he grabbed Lanaya from her arms and then Keikeo.

"Kash, we are not about to do this. You fucked up not me," Nae said as the tears fell. She was pissed because she didn't want him seeing her cry.

"Nae, I did fuck up and I'm willing to do anything to fix it," Kash said willing to beg.

"You can start by leaving me the fuck alone. This so called relationship we had is over," Nae said as she brushed pass him running off.

"Mommy, crying," Keikeo said pointing to Nae.

Kash was torn inside and out, his world had just crashed right before his eyes and he didn't know if he could fix it. His kissed the twins before putting them down to continuing playing. Lanaya went back to playing and Keikeo ran after Nae.

*

Nae paced back and forth crying. Kash didn't know how bad he had just crushed her and ripped her heart into two. Fuck two; he had shattered her heart into a million little pieces. "I can't do this," Nae mumbled as she continued to cry. Nae looked at her ring; she played with it for a while before sliding it off her finger. She sat it on the dresser walking away. She didn't know if she could bounce back from this. Kash had did the unthinkable and slept with another bitch. Something she couldn't and wouldn't tolerate. She felt if he did it once he'll do it again. It was unacceptable, it didn't matter what the reason was.

"Mommy, don't cry," Keikeo said standing in the door way.

"Come here baby," Nae said as she held her arms out from her little prince. Keikeo walked over to Nae and she picked him up, hugging him tightly. Keikeo looked at Nae before using his small hands to wipe her tears away.

"I love you, mommy," he said kissing her on her check. Nae smiled.

"I love you too," she said back. Nae heart ached her home had just split into two.

*

Kash sat watching Lanaya play. Once again his life was falling apart. He didn't know the outcome of this problem but he was praying it all ended well. Kash reached into his pocket for his cell. He dialed his nigga, Jacques up.

"Speak on it," Ques answered his phone.

"Bruh, shit is all bad," Kash said into the phone.

"What happened now?" Jacques asked. It was as if Kash and Nae weren't meant to be together. Every time they turned around something was happening.

"I told her," Kash answered running his hands over his face. "I fucked up."

"My nigga you did fuck up. The only thing I can tell you is to fight for ya relationship," Jacques said. "It isn't gonna be easy but if Nae is who you really wanna be with you gotta show her." He finished.

"Fuck! Why me?" Kash asked.

"Nigga, that's an answer neither of us have. Just do what you gotta do to keep your lady," Jacques said. He knew the situation all too well.

Keikeo came running into the room. "Da-da, mommy leaving," he said pointing to the door as he jumped on Kash lap.

"I'm gonna call you back," he said into the phone before hanging up. Kash stood to his feet in a hurried to catch up with Nae.

"Bye-Bye, mommy," Lanaya said still playing with her toys.

*

"Nae!" Kash called just as she was opening the front door. Nae continued walking ignoring his calls. "Nae, stop," Kash said as he put Keikeo down to go after her. He grabbed her just before she could step outside. Turning her around to face him, he found her face covered with tears. Kash sighed as he tried to wipe her tears away but Nae turned her face away.

"Kash, I can't do this right now," she whispered never looking in his eyes. "Maybe this isn't meant to be."

"Nae, I respect that fact that you may need time and some space but what we have is meant to be," Kash said.

"How could you say that? When you stepped out on me?" She asked.

"It's something I didn't wanna do-"

"But you did and I can't live with that. How would you feel if I stepped out on you?" She asked causing Kash to frown. "My point," Nae said as she turned to walk away.

Kash grabbed her left hand; he looked down when he didn't feel her engagement ring on her finger causing his heart to ache. Nae slipped her hand from Kash walking off.

"Bye-bye mommy," Keikeo said waving as he laid his head on Kash leg.

"Mommy will be back. I promise," Nae said turning to look in her son's handsome face.

*

Nae got in her car closing the door behind her. She slumped in her seat sighing deeply. She remembered when she said she wouldn't shed anymore tears for Kash and here she was once again crying over him. Yes, she loved him but cheating was something she couldn't deal with. She hadn't given him a reason to but yet and still he did. She made sure she had his food cooked and waiting for him. She give him pussy whenever he asked for it, she washed his clothes and took care of their kids. What more could any man ask for from a woman?

Nae started her car with no real destination in mind. All she knew was that she needed to get away to clear her mind. Her heart ached for leaving her babies but it was something she had to do for now.

"UGH, I fuckin' hate him," Nae said banging her fist into the steering wheel. "Maria out of all the bitches he could have he picks her?" Nae asked. *"Oh that bitch will die this go 'round."* She thought pulling out of her driveway. Nae looked in her rearview mirror as the home she had grown to love faded in the distances.

*

Kash wasn't at all surprised at the fact that Nae left. It hurt him, but he knew telling her was something he had to do. Kash rather Nae find out by him and not by word of mouth from someone else. He had taken a huge risk at gambling and was on the verge of losing everything he had worked so hard to get. Material things were something Kash never worried about because he knew it came and went. Material things could always get replaced but love, the love him and Nae had for one and other was something you only found once in a life time. Kash had just watched his love walk out their front door.

Chapter Five

Anna walked around the mall doing a little window shopping. Shopping was something she loved to do during her free time. She wore a smile on her face as Jacques came to mind. It had been years since they were in the same room let alone her getting some dick from him. Anna closed her eyes as she bit into her bottom lip. Just the thought of Jacques fucking her had her pussy over flowing. Her smile quickly faded as Cherry came to mind. She was in her way. She saw the way Jacques looked at her or held her close when they were out or lying in bed together. Anna knew the only way to get Jacques back was to take Cherry out and she had no problem doing just that. She would do just about anything to have him back in her life. Anna had always been obsessed with him. Since she could remember.

Anna walked pass the Gucci store and had to do a double take. She admired the lady standing there looking over different items. Anna took her in from head to toe and had to admit that she was indeed a bad bitch. The way she walked and dressed let Anna know that she was a classy chick. The diamonds she wore also let Anna know that she was also a getting money bitch. Before Anna knew it, she found herself walking into the Gucci store with her eyes glued on the woman as she admired her some more.

"Mommy, can I get these?" Jewel asked holding up a pair of brown and pink Gucci sneakers. "Oh, mommy I have to have these too," she said waving a pair of Gucci logo baby doll shoes in the air. Anna smiled at the gorgeous little girl with a head full of ponytails.

Cherry laughed. "Jewel, you can have one so pick," Cherry said causing her to poke her bottom lip out.

"Mommy," Jewel wined folding her arms across her chest.

"Okay, you can get them both," Cherry laughed again. How could she deny her baby girl anything?

"Thank you," Jewel smiled as she jumped up and down.

Cherry could feel someone looking at her so she looked up to find a lady staring at her and Jewel.

"You have a gorgeous little girl," Anna smiled.

"Thanks," replied Cherry as she gave Anna a funny look. Something was off about this lady but she shook it off as her and Jewel continued to have their mother daughter outing.

Anna stood there as she tried to figure out just what it was that Cherry possess that she didn't to capture Jacques heart.

The small hand tapping her leg drew her attention. She looked down to find Jewel waving and smiling at her. "Hi," Anna smiled.

"Jewel, bring ya ass over here," Cherry said. Jewel waved bye as she skipped over to where Cherry stood.

"Excuse me but I'm starting to feel some type of way and believe me you don't want that," she assured looking Anna up and down.

Anna and Cherry stood there staring each other down before Anna backed off. "I didn't think so," Cherry said rolling her eyes before turning to finishing her shopping.

"We will be seeing a lot more of each other," Anna mumbled with a smile sitting on her face. She turned to walk out of the store.

*

Jacques stood off to the corner as he watched JJ standing in the middle of the boxing ring practicing his moves. "Lil' nigga stick and move," Jacques coached JJ. "Bob and weave," he continued to coach his baby boy. JJ was only four years old but his fighting game was already up to par. With a little more practice he would be ill with his hands.

Jacques had JJ in boxing, basketball and football. He wanted his little nigga in sports far away from the streets.

"Take a break," the coach said. JJ hung his head low as he walked towards Jacques breathing heavily.

"Why are you walking with your head hung low?" Ques asked.

"Daddy, I can't-"

"Fuck you mean you can't?" Ques asked. "What I tell you about using that word?"

"Sorry, but he's too big," JJ huffed as Jacques gave him a drink of water.

"Sit down," Ques said feeling some type of way about what JJ had just said.

"Listen, it doesn't matter how big or small your opponent is. They bleed and fall just as you do," he assured. "You just have to go in there with your all. Win, lose, or draw, as long as you show up and show out. Make 'em respect you for you," Jacques said to his four year old son. He wasn't sure if he understood any of it as long as he went out there showing no fear.

"Let's go," the coach said. Jacques rubbed the top of JJ's head telling him to get back in the ring and to give his all. JJ climbed back into the ring ready. He turned to look at Jacques who gave him a head nod.

Jacques didn't understand how any father could walk out on their kids especially their sons. He loved everything about being a father. It had its ups and downs but that was part of life. *"Damn, I almost missed out on raising my kids."* He thought rubbing his chest.

Jacques reached in his pocket for his ringing phone.

"Talk to me." He answered keeping his eyes glued on his son.

"Hi daddy," Anna said. Jacques sighed as he grabbed his dreads.

"How do you get my number and what do you want?" He asked letting her know just how annoyed he was with her playing on his phone.

"You daddy," she replied.

"Not gonna happen."

"Guess who I ran into today?" She asked. He could tell she was smiling on the other end of the phone.

"I really don't give a fuck who you ran into today," he said ready to hang up.

"Are you sure about that? I ran into ya little girl friend today," she said getting his attention now. Jacques sighed while running his hands over his face.

"Correction bitch, that's my fiancée," Jacques spat. "Something you will never be."

"Once again are you sure about that?" Anna asked.

"I'm sure about that."

"She's cute. I'll give her that." Jacques laughed.

"My shawty is one of the baddest if not the baddest," he corrected her once again. "Check this shit out. Stop callin' and playing on my phone and whatever it is that you have planned please dead it because you don't want these problems." Jacques said hanging up on Anna.

Before Jacques, could slide his phone back into his pocket it rung again.

"What?" He answered.

"Fuck wrong with you?" Cherry asked.

"My bad ma, mothafuckas playing on my phone," he answered. "What's good, where you at?"

"I'm in the mall-"

"You mind as well build ya own fuckin' mall. Cause you stay in that bitch," Jacques laughed.

"Whatever, you don't be saying that shit when I buy all those damn teddies and costumes you like," laughed

Cherry as she playfully rolled her eyes.

"You damn right, speaking of which, I hope you copped a few," Jacques laughed.

"Nope, what time will you be home?" Cherry asked.

"As soon as JJ finish practice and don't try changing the subject," Jacques said. "You better march ya ass back in that mall and grab me something I can take off you tonight."

"Bye Ques. I'll see you when you get home," Cherry said disconnecting the call.

Jacques turned just in time to see JJ knock his opponent on his ass. "That's what the fuck I'm talkin' about!" Jacques yelled with his hands in the air.

"I did it. Did you see me knock his ass out?" JJ asked. Ques had to hold his laugh back.

"Lil nigga watch ya mouth," Ques said with a finger in his face. "Go give him a pound so we can go."

JJ did what he was told before walking back to his father. Jacques smiled as he helped remove the boxing gloves. "Give me some," he said as they slapped hands.

"I told you you could do it," Ques said as they exit the building.

"I knocked his big ass out," JJ stated proudly.

This time Ques laughed. "Watch ya damn mouth," Jacques warned once again.

"I'm hungry," JJ said as they got into the car.

"What you wanna eat?"

"McDonald's," answered JJ. Jacques shook his head. That's all JJ and Jewel ever wanted to eat.

"Daddy, I gotta call my uncles to tell them they ain't messing with my right jab," JJ smiled throwing his hands to block his face as if he was back in the ring.

Jacques laughed. "We'll call them niggas when we get home," he said pulling into traffic.

*

Cherry cursed herself for over doing it in the mall once again. She tried balancing Jewel in one arm while carrying all their bags. Jewel wasn't making it any better as she wiggled and giggled at whatever had her attention behind them.

"Bye-Bye," Jewel said waving.

"Who are you talkin' too?" Cherry asked looking over her shoulders. Jewel giggled as she pointed behind them. Cherry stopped walking to see just who it was but found everyone going about their business. Cherry knew Jewel had a crazy imagination but damn. Cherry didn't know that Jewel wasn't imaging anything she was talking to Anna who had been following their every move since they had left out of the Gucci store.

Cherry struggled out the mall barely making it to her car, which was parked half way down the parking lot. Cherry finally made it to her car. Sitting the bags and Jewel down she searched her purse for her car keys. Grabbing her keys she popped the trunk putting her bags inside with help from Jewel of course. "Thank you," Cherry said as she closed the trunk walking around the car to help Jewel into her car seat.

"Mommy, I'm hungry," Jewel said biting her nails. Cherry popped her hand. Jewel started crying as if she had just gotten the ass whooping of her life.

"Really, Jewel?" Cherry asked making sure she was strapped in before closing the door walking to the driver side getting in. "What do you wanna eat?" She asked looking into the rearview mirror at Jewel who still was crying.

"Chicken nuggets," Jewel perked up smiling. "Mommy, cut that up," Jewel said as Super Bass by Nicki Minaj spilled from the speakers. Cherry laughed as she watched Jewel try singing along. Cherry backed her car out of the parking space heading for McDonald's.

*

Anna kept a low profile as she followed Cherry thru the mall. She had been doing great until her daughter waved saying bye bye to her. She had to dip into a nearby store as Cherry turned to see who she was talking too. Anna didn't want to blow her cover just yet. In due time her and Cherry would meet again and it wasn't gonna end well for one of them. "That little girl is very observant," Anna said as she sat behind the wheel of her car. She was surprised she didn't remember her from the day she stood outside their home.

Anna stood in front of the door battling with herself wondering if she should knock or not. She had seen when Cherry got into the taxi. She knew she was on her way out of town from the suit cases she had placed in the trunk. This was the first time Anna was seeing Cherry up close and personal. She didn't want to admit it and she would never admit it to anyone but she envied Cherry and she didn't know her from a hole in a wall.

Anna pulled her eyes from Cherry and let them scan over Jacques entire body. "Damn, he's still sexy." She thought biting into her bottom lip. Anna watched their every move. She could tell Jacques was very much in love. The love was seeping from his pours and she could feel it from her car parked across the street, causing Anna to wonder why he never loved her like that.

"Finally!" Anna thought as she watched Jacques tap the top of the cab and it slowly began pulling off. Jacques stood there watching until the cab disappeared down the street before he turned to his son going back into the house.

Anna argued with herself for a while before she found herself getting out of her car walking right up to his front door. Before she could knock on the door it opened up. Jacques walked out holding both his kids.

"Jacques," Anna called him getting his attention. Jacques turned around.

"Anna? The fuck are you doin' here?" He asked looking around.

"I told you I want you back," she answered taking a step closer to him.

"Back the fuck up," he said putting his kids down.

"Baby, I'm back," Anna said holding her arms out.

"Where are you back from? The dead?" He asked. "It's been how long since we last seen or even talked to each other?" He fired off.

"No, not from the dead, Ques, they locked me up in the nut house," Anna said.

"They should have kept you there. Because you have got to be crazy showing up to my home like it's okay," Jacques spat as he picked he kids up carrying them to the car.

Anna laughed. "Jacques, I see you are the one to still speak your mind."

"Always, that will never change," he said strapping JJ and Jewel into their car seats. He closed the door behind him before facing Anna. He looked her up and down and had to admit that she was looking damn good. He quickly shook the thoughts because he had who he wanted there wasn't ever any need for him to step out.

If Jacques didn't know any better he would have said it was good seeing her but he didn't want to give her any wrong ideas. After all, the bitch had just informed him of her being in a nut house. And if that wasn't enough evidence to confirm that she was missing a few screws, the fact that she was standing in the front of his home said it all.

"Jacques, we need to talk," Anna said grabbing his arm.

"We don't need to talk about shit," he spat snatching he arm back. "Whatever you thought dead that shit. I'm happy as you can see." He said pointing around.

"What about us?"

"There isn't an us. We use to fuck around when we were teens-"

"How could you say that? You use to always tell me you loved me," Anna said holding back the tears.

"Bitch, that was me tryna get some pussy. After all you had the best shit back then," he laughed as he walked around his car to get in.

Jacques chucked up the deuces before climbing into his car.

Anna couldn't believe he had just played her the way he had, as if they didn't have a past.

Anna cracked a small smile as she thought on a plan to get Jacques in her bed. She caught him licking his lips causing her to close her eyes imagining his tongue all over her body. "Ummm," she moaned squeezing her legs together.

They locked eyes one last time as Jacques left her standing there.

Anna felt the tingle between her legs knowing she would have to please herself when she got home later on that night. *"That will have to do until I get Jacques in my bed."* She thought starting her car pulling off.

*

Cherry pulled up the McDonald's driver thru. After placing her order she drove to the first window to pay for her order and then pulled to the second window to wait for her order. She was happy that she wouldn't have to wait long.

When she looked up she saw Jacques standing in line

ordering his food. She smiled because she wasn't expecting to see him. Her smile faded just as quickly as it had formed when she saw a lady approach Jacques. It was cool for him to talk to whomever he wanted but the bitch was becoming a little too hands on for Cherry liking. Cherry quickly pulled from the drive-thru line to find a parking spot so that she could go inside forgetting all about Jewel's happy meal.

"Mommy, my nuggets," Jewel pouted. Cherry ignored her as she parked the car. Getting out she opened the back door to help Jewel from her car seat. She rushed inside with Jewel glued to her hip. As she walked thru the dining area she could see Jacques and the unknown woman having a deep conversation, her hand rubbing up and down his back as if he was her man.

"Aww, he's too cute," she said. "I wonder where he gets he looks from." She laughed squeezing Jacques arm.

"Ma, stop it. You see where he gets his looks from," Jacques said.

"You ain't ever lied," she said. "I see good looks run in the family."

"They damn sure do," Cherry said finally ending their conversation. Jacques turned around to find Cherry standing there with a pissed off look on her face.

"Fuck you come from?" He asked taking a step back.

"Don't worry about it. What's this?" Cherry asked pointing to the lady as she looked her up and down.

"Nothing, we were just holding a conversation about JJ,"

answered Ques.

"From what I could see, this bitch was tryna hold more than a conversation," Cherry said.

Jacques sucked his teeth. "Chill out, ma. It ain't that serious. I already know what I got at home," Ques said wrapping his arms around Cherry.

"My bad I didn't know he was taken. I liked what I saw so I went for it," the lady said smiling at Jacques.

"Bitch you better go head, while ya ass can still walk out on your own," Cherry warned putting Jewel down.

"Cherry chill damn, what's wrong with you?" Jacques asked.

"Oh I see what this is. She's scared of a little competition," the lady said. Cherry laughed.

"Girl bye, I killed my competition years ago. You hoes ain't fuckin' with me," Cherry smiled. "You can't fuck with me if I gave you 101 lessons on how to." Cherry finished.

"Ma'am, your happy meal," the worker said walking over to Cherry.

"Thanks," she replied as she handed Jewel her happy meal bag. "And just to show you that you ain't fuckin' with me, here's ya chance to try and get what's mine," Cherry said as she grabbed Jewel hand walking away. "Good luck," she called over her shoulders.

Jacques stood there tryna figure out what had happened.

"Like I was saying before she interrupted us-"

"Ma, there's no need in trying. I'm already taken." Jacques said cutting her short. "It was nice talkin' to you though." He said grabbing him and JJ's dinner for the night.

Jacques stepped outside scanning the McDonald's parking lot until his eyes fell on Cherry's pink Benz. He strolled over to it tapping on her window. She rolled down the window smiling.

"Mommy," JJ said leaning into the window hugging her around her neck.

"Hi baby. How was practice?" She asked.

"I kicked his big ass," JJ beamed. Cherry laughed.

"What I tell you about your mouth?" Jacques asked him.

"Sorry, I kicked his big butt," JJ corrected as Jacques placed him in the back seat with Jewel.

"Hi daddy," she waved eating her chicken nuggets.

"Hi princess, what was all that for?" He asked turning his attention to Cherry.

"All what?" She asked smiling.

"How many times do I have to tell you that you don't have to worry about the next bitch? I know what I got at home," He said leaning in kissing her lips.

"Ewwww," JJ and Jewel said laughing.

"I'm not worrying about a damn thing. I just don't like bitches all up on what belongs to me," Cherry said.

"Ma, they can't help but to be all up on me. Look at me,"

Jacques laughed taking a step back patting his chest. His NY swag was on blast for all to see with his dreads in a ponytail. "Ladies can't get enough of me."

"Fall back with ya cocky ass," Cherry laughed starting her ride. "I'll see you when you get home."

"A'ight, be safe ma," Ques said pecking Cherry on the lips before walking to his own car.

Chapter Six

Nae didn't know what else to do or where else to go and before she knew it she found herself buying a plane ticket to New Orleans. Nae knew New Orleans would be the last place Kash looked for her. She stepped out the rental, taking a deep breath she made her way to the door. She knew Ray was home because she and Melo cars were parked out front. She rung the door bell and waited for Ray to answer.

"Who the fuck knocking on my door?" Melo asked as he unlocked the door. Nae didn't bother answering him.

He opened the door. "Oh, what the fuck happen to you?" He asked holding his gun to his side.

"Man, move and shut ya punk ass up," Nae said rolling her eyes as she brushed pass him. Where's Ray?"

"She's dressing up for our little role play you interrupted," Melo answered closing the door behind them. He removed the blunt from behind his ear to light it. "Here, it looks like you need this." He laughed.

"Nigga, shut up," Nae said cracking a small smile taking the blunt he was offering.

"Melo, shut up," Ray said coming into view. "Your ass ain't getting any pussy," Ray informed him smiling.

"Tuh! You a lie," he said walking pass smacking Ray on the ass.

Ray flipped him off as she looked at Nae. "What

happened?" She asked as they walked into the kitchen. Ray was excited to see her bitch but from the way Nae looked she could tell this wasn't a social call at all. Nae burst into tears.

"Ray, he cheated on me," Nae said wiping the tears away.

"Aye, it looks like its murking season," Ray said. "Where that nigga at?"

"I left him home. But you will never guess with who," Nae said puffing on the blunt.

"Who, I hope not one of them off brand bitches."

"Maria."

"Maria, Maria why that name sound so familiar?" Ray asked mumbling that name over and over. "Isn't that the bitch you sliced up a few years ago?" She asked snapping her fingers. Nae nodded her head up and down.

"Oh bitch, it's on. Fuck is she at?" Ray asked. "It's murking season, New Orleans style."

Nae knew Ray would be down for whatever. All her girls would be after they tried talking her out of leaving Kash. But there was no way in hell she could stay with him at this point. "I love him but this shit cut me deep," Nae said shaking her head.

"Seriously, Nae, you and Kash has been thru hell and back. Are you willing to throw what you two have built over this, away?" Ray asked as she walked around the kitchen grabbing two glasses and a bottle of Hennessy. She knew her girl needed a stiff drink. "He could have kept it from you. At least he was man enough to let you know what was goin' on."

"Bitch, he fucked the next bitch and told me he did it for us," Nae spat. "Where the fuck they do that at?"

"Wow," Ray said. That was her first time ever hearing anything like that. "How long have this been goin' on?" Nae shrugged her shoulders. She really didn't care because it shouldn't have been going on in the first place.

"I really don't know." Nae said. I just know that I'm moving on." she shrugged her shoulders.

"Nae, you're really goin' to let go that easy?" Ray asked seeing the hurt her girl was carrying in her eyes.

"I rather let go than get my heart crushed over and over again," Nae answered. "From here on out the only thing Kamil and I have to talk about are our kids."

"Excuse me," Melo said walking into the kitchen. "Ray, let a nigga holla at you," he said waving her over.

"What?" Ray asked.

"Are y'all done talkin'?" He asked.

"No, my girl needs me," Ray said.

"Shit we need you too," he said pointing to himself as he looked down at his dick. Ray laughed waving him off.

"Boy bye. You'll be alright," Ray said turning to walk away.

"So that's how it is? You just gonna leave a nigga on hard times?" He asked. Nae rolled her eyes while Ray ignored him.

"Ray, I'm gonna go take a bath and lay down," Nae said as she slipped from the stool she was sitting on. She turned on her heels to grab the bottle of Hennessy she would be drowning her sorrows in for the night.

"Are you sure?" Ray asked.

"Yeah she sure," Melo jumped in.

"Shut up fool," Ray spat. Nae laughed.

"I'm sure, go handle ya business," Nae said as she pointed to Melo. "Thank you." She said taking the blunt resting between Melo's lips.

"Come on son," Melo said throwing his hands in the air. Nae flipped him off as she made her way upstairs. He laughed. "Right back at cha. Now you, come handle ya business like she said," he said turning to face Ray.

Ray grabbed her cup walking pass Melo. "Where are you goin'?"

"To watch a movie," Ray said over her shoulders.

"That's what you think," he said walking to the fridge grabbing a hand full of ice. He grabbed him a cup before following Ray to their bedroom.

*

Kash stood in the middle of the living room watching his babies sleep. It had been a long day for them all. He had been tempted to call Nae but he decided against it. He knew she needed her space. He respected that, giving her time to think and figure out just what she wanted to do. *"I fucked up."* He thought picking Keikeo and Lanaya up carrying them to their rooms. He laid them down and tucked them in before he turned the lights out and closed the door behind him.

Kash walked to his bedroom, flicking the light on he looked around. It had only been a few hours but it already felt empty. Her ring sitting on the dresser caught his attention. He walked over to the dresser picking it up. He admired the purple diamond. It didn't matter if they ended up back together or not, Kash felt Nae deserved the ring. She had done more than her part earning any and everything he had given her. Kash never meant to cause Nae any type of pain. He just wanted to treat her the way she was supposed to be treated and live happily ever after. Since, Kash could remember, luck and love has never been on his side. Kash kissed the purple diamond as he reached into his pocket for his cell. He needed to hear her voice. Before he could dial her number his phone rang.

"Hello?" He answered.

"Hi papi," Maria said into the phone.

"Why are you callin' my phone?"

"I called to see if you came to ya senses yet?" She asked laughing.

"Listen, this so called game you was playing is over. She knows everything," Kash spat annoyed. Because of this bitch he was on the verge of losing everything that matter the most to him.

"Kash, this game isn't over until I defeat my opponents," Maria said. Kash chuckled.

"We are undefeatable," he said. "Good luck though." He said hanging up on her. Kash knew he would have to kill her soon. What he didn't know was that Maria had already begun her games, games that would tear his world apart.

Kash stared at his phone for a while before finally dialing Nae's number. Hitting talk he placed the phone to his ear waiting for the call to connect and for her to answer.

Kash sighed as he hung up just to redial her number. He didn't want to hear her voicemail. He wanted to hear her voice and would continue calling until she decided to answer her phone or it went dead, whichever came first.

*

Nae soaked in a tub filled with hot water and bubbles as Mary soulful voice played in the background. Nae knew that it was time for her to move on. She thought that she had found true love only to be fooled once again. This go round she was locking her heart up. She rather be lonely than to keep letting niggas hurt her. Nae's phone rang. She looked at the caller ID to find Kash picture flashing across the screen with the word Hubby going across it. She ignored the call. She couldn't take hearing his voice. She knew they would have to talk about it eventually but it wasn't time for that. She let it go to voicemail. A few seconds later it was ringing and once again it was Kash. This time she answered thinking about her babies. "Hello?" She answered.

"Where are you?"

"About my business, is my babies okay?" She asked.

"Fuck kind of question is that? Yeah they okay," Kash spat.

"We need to talk."

"Kash, the only things we need to every talk about is our kids. If it doesn't pertain to them we don't have shit to talk about," she said matching his tone of voice.

"I'm fuckin' sorry. Nae, I can't lose you," Kash said.

"Nigga, if you didn't do what you did you wouldn't have to say sorry," Nae spat. "You fucked up what we had and for what?" She asked. "Oh yeah that's right you did it for us, right?" She laughed.

"Nae, at that point in time I didn't think I had a choice. I was protecting you," Kash said.

"Protecting me from what? If that bitch wanted to do something she would have done it years ago. She got what she wanted and that was you," Nae said. "How long have this been goin' on?" She asked closing her eyes. She was afraid of hearing the answer but it was too late she had already asked the question.

"How long?" She asked again when Kash didn't answer.

"Over a year."

"WHAT? You've been fuckin' the hoe for over a year behind my back?" Nae asked disgusted. "Fuck you Kash. I hope she was worth it." Nae said hanging up on him. She refused to cry anymore. It was what it was. Nae washed her body and rinsed off before getting out. Grabbing her towel she wrapped herself in it before leaving the bathroom.

Nae stopped in her tracks hearing the head board banging against to wall and Ray moaning. "Okay." She said as she grabbed the remote turning the radio up hoping it would help tune Ray and Melo asses out.

Kash has just unleashed the old Nae, the one who didn't give a fuck about anybody but herself. Treating niggas how they treated bitches. She was about to show mothafuckas how you play with someone's heart and emotions.

*

Kash knew things between him and Nae was over but he wasn't gonna stop fighting for their relationship. They had weathered one storm he knew they could weather this one. To him fighting for their relationship was worth it all. Nae was the only female to capture his heart. He needed her just as much as he needs air to breathe. She was his better half. He just had to work twice as hard to prove that he was worth fighting for.

Kash closed his eyes hoping sleep would consume him quickly. This was only the first night of him not sleeping with Nae. He knew it would be plenty more nights like this, something he couldn't get use too. Before long Kash was sleep with Nae heavy on his brain.

"DADDDDDYYYYYYYYY!" Lanaya screamed waking Kash from his sleep. He jumped from his bed rushing out of his room.

"DON'T MOVE!" He heard stopping in his tracks.

"What the fuck goin' on?" Kash asked as he held his hands in the air. He was surrounded by Cali's finest. "The fuck are y'all doin' in my home?" He asked as he listened to Keikeo and Lanaya screaming and reaching out for him.

"Get on the ground!" Another officer yelled.

"For what?" Kash asked as his eyes darted across the hall. He had no idea as to why they were in his home and he wanted answers. "Why are y'all in my home?"

"Get the fuck down!" They begin to scream. Kash finally did as he was told only so his kids didn't have to witness him getting an ass whipping by the police for not doing what he was told.

"Is any of you mothafuckas gonna tell me what's goin' on?" Kash asked as they rushed him to cuff his hands behind his back.

"Daddy," Lanaya cried.

"Baby, stop crying. I'm right here," Kash said trying his best to calm her down.

"Search the entire house," The Detective said.

"For what? What are you lookin' for?" Kash asked as he was being helped to his feet.

"Mr. Washington, we have a warrant to search your home. We were tipped that there was drugs being stored here," the Detective said.

"Drugs?" Kash asked with a confused look on his face. He hadn't sold drugs in years and he was smart enough to not keep drugs where he rested his head.

"Well you better check ya sources because they're fuckin' wrong," Kash gritted.

"Mr. Washington, welcome to California," Detective

Morris laughed patting him on his back before walking away.

Lanaya got loose from the officer holding her running to Kash wrapping her little arms around his leg. Kash was beyond pissed. He never wanted his kids to go through what they were going through. Kash stopped the officer coming after Lanaya as he stood with his chest poked out. "Don't touch my daughter, Keikeo, come here," Kash said never taking his eyes of the police officer standing in front of him. Kash didn't stop staring him down until Keikeo and Lanaya was both standing behind him. Kash turned around to talk to his kids but was hit with a powerful blow to the back of his head.

"Aaaahhh!" He screamed before dropping to the floor passing out.

"Daddy!" Lanaya and Keikeo screamed as tears cascaded down their little faces. Their cries went on death ears as the officers went about searching their home.

Kash was awakening when someone poured a cold glass of water on his face. "Aahh," he said as he shook his head. At first everything was a blur. The splitting headache that ripped thru his head caused him to stop any movement he was doing. That didn't last long as he looked around for his kids. Finally his eyes came into focus.

"Didn't I tell you I was goin' to make your life a living hell?" Maria asked standing over Kash with a wicked grin sitting on her face. "And didn't I tell you that I run shit now?" She asked.

"Aahh, you know you're dead right?" Kash asked as pain ripped thru his head.

Maria laughed, "If you say so. Welcome to Cali, Kash," she said turning to walk away. "Oh before I forget tell that bitch of yours that she's next." Kash laid his head back breathing heavily. He knew without a doubt, killing Maria was a must. She had crossed the line involving his kids. "Un-cuff him and let's go," Kash heard Maria said.

Kash heard the footsteps before long he was roughly being picked up. He slowly opened his eyes to take in as many of their faces as he could. Kash was sure about one thing, they would all pay for violating his babies. That was a big NO-NO and death was the only thing he could think to do. He was getting ready to show them what was to happen when they fucked with him.

"Maria!" Kash called as they un-cuffed him. She stopped turning to see just what he wanted. She found a slight grin sitting on his face. "Thanks for the welcome to Cali," Kash winked sending chills down her back. "You're gonna wish you never did that," he said with coldness dripping from his voice. Maria looked at him smiling.

"Let the games begin," she said waving bye.

Kash watched as they left him home in a shamble. None of that mattered as he walked over to his twins to make sure they were unharmed. Despite the pain he felt in his head it could never compare to the pain he felt in his heart. He had been trying to keep the old Kash caged up. He had been doing well for the past two years but all that changed that night. He sure as hell was getting ready to show Cali and their police department what he was made of. Kash picked his babies up hugging them tightly.

"Daddy, you're bleeding," Keikeo said seeing the blood

leaking from Kash head.

Kash didn't care too much about the gash in the back of his head.

He sat them back on the bed so that he could grab his phone. He dialed a number hitting talk.

"Yo?" Shyne answered.

"My nigga it's war. I'm 'bout to turn this mothafuckin' city inside out," Kash said.

"What happen?" Shyne asked all ears.

"I'll fill you in later. I'm taking my babies to New York just be ready when I get back," Kash said disconnecting the call.

Kash could have easily called his niggas up. He didn't wanna involve any of them. They had left the game alone years ago. This was his problem so he had to handle it by himself.

Kash went into the bathroom to clean himself up before dressing Keikeo and Lanaya. Before long he was out the door.

*

Shyne looked at the phone wondering just what the hell was going on with Kash. He could tell by the tone of his voice that things weren't good.

"Is everything okay?" Kendra asked as she sat up to face Shyne.

"For now it is," Shyne answered as he pulled her onto his

chest as he laid back down.

Lately he and Kendra had been spending a lot of time together. He loved everything about her. Love was something Shyne wasn't looking for up until he had met Kendra. She didn't know it but she even had him considering leaving the game alone. *"She gotta be the one."* He thought playing in her hair.

"Hello, what has ya mind?" Kendra asked.

"You," replied Shyne.

"That was a hell of an answer but I'm being serious," she said lifting her head so that she could look at him.

"I'm serious. I haven't been close to a woman like this in a while. It feels good," laughed Shyne. "Around this time I'm use to sending them on home."

"You niggas kill me."

"Aww shit here we go," Shyne laughed.

"No for real. Y'all niggas always hollering about wanting a good girl but when y'all get 'em y'all treat 'em like shit and expect them to stay enduring all the pain y'all cause for a fuckin' image," Kendra said.

"It's hard to find a good woman now days. Most are blinded by the life style us niggas live. Half y'all don't be in love with us for us. Y'all asses are in love with our money and what we can do for you," Shyne shot back.

"Tuh, that's those bitches y'all attract because that's what y'all look for. You get what you put out," Kendra said.

"Well I'm tryna put out love what's up?" He asked. Kendra lowered her head. "Nah ma, talk to me."

"Shyne, I'm feeling you I just don't wanna get hurt," Kendra answered. "It always starts like this. Too good to be true then boom a year in the real you comes out."

"Ken this is me all day every day. I will never hurt you, I got you," he tried to assure.

Kendra laid her head back on his chest as she thought on what he had just asked. Shyne was cool, smart, handsome, and a thug. She knew how it ended with niggas like him. They played with ya emotions got you all strung out and leaves you for the next bitch. It was already too late because she had already falling into deep. The feelings she had for Shayne was more than she showed. The way he showered her with love and affection, held her and talked to her with so much care in the world. He made it a point in calling her at least six times a day just to see how her day was going.

"You don't ever have to worry about getting hurt as long as I live," Shyne whispered in her ear before kissing the top of her head.

"I sure hope so," Kendra said.

Chapter Seven

Jacques opened his eyes looking around. His house was to quiet letting him know Cherry had taken the kids with her. *"Good, a nigga can sleep in."* Jacques thought closing his eyes.

"Good morning, I hope you're hungry," Anna said.

Jacques jumped from his bed to find Anna holding a tray full of breakfast goods.

"Yo, how did you get in my house?" He asked.

"It was easy," she smiled sitting his plate on the bed beside him. "By the way your alarm system sucks," she giggled walking away as if she belonged there.

"You gotta go," Jacques said in search of his clothes.

"Oh baby what's the rush. Cherry isn't gonna be back anytime soon," she said taking a seat crossing her legs.

"What the fuck do you want?" Jacques asked.

"You," she replied licking her lips.

"Not gonna happen," he said shaking his head. "Get the fuck out!" He ordered her as he slipped into his sweats.

"What's the rush?" Anna smiled. "WE have all day."

Jacques wasn't up for the games and wanted her out now. He rushed over to her forcefully grabbing her by the arm yanking her from her seat.

"Mmmm, I like playing rough," she giggled as he pulled her out his room and down the stairs.

"Listen, I don't know how you found me or why you ever came lookin' for me but I'm not with these games. Go find someone else to fuck with," he gritted.

"But I don't want anybody else. It's you I want and I'm not gonna stop until I have you," she said.

"Anna, listen to me," Jacques said shaking the shit out of her hoping to knock some sense into that empty head of hers. "There will never be us. I'm happy where I am." He said opening the door to find, Cherry getting ready to unlock the door. "FUCK!" He yelled shaking his head.

"Excuse me, what's goin' on here?" Cherry asked looking from Jacques to Anna. "You're the bitch from the mall." Cherry said as Anna smiled.

"So we meet again," Anna said.

"It isn't what you think," Jacques quickly said.

"Daddy that's the lady from when we were leaving to see auntie Nae," Jewel said pointing to Anna.

"JJ, take Jewel in the other room to play," Jacques said. JJ grabbed his little sister walking off.

"So you're keeping secrets again?" Cherry asked ignoring Anna standing there.

"No, I was gonna tell you-"

"When?" Cherry asked trying to stay as calm as she could. Secrets are what had almost cost Jacques to lose her in the first place. She didn't keep anything from him and she expected nothing less from him. "How long has this been goin' on?"

"A while," replied Anna. Cherry cut her eye at her.

"There's nothing goin' on," Jacques said. "This bitch is stalking me. That's all that's goin' on." Cherry halt off smacking the shit out of Anna, hitting her so hard spit flew from her mouth. She turned and smacked the shit out of Jacques.

"What the fuck was that for?" He asked holding his burning cheek. "Girl, you got power behind them little ass hands of yours." He said pissed.

Cherry ignored him putting her attention back on Anna. "Bitch, I don't know what it is that you want or what made you decide to fuck with him. But this isn't what you wanna do," Cherry warned.

"Oh but it is. I've been in love with, Jacques since I can remember," Anna said still holding her cheek with a smile sitting upon her lips. "And I'm willing to do just about *anything* to get him back." She finished. She could tell Cherry was gonna be more of a challenge after all. There wasn't anything wrong with one, was it? All the mattered was who came out on top with the prize.

Cherry punched Anna in the face with a vicious blow causing her head to jerk back. "Oh shit," Jacques said as he stepped in the middle. Anna put her hand to her face removing it to find blood on her hand. She laughed as she licked the blood from her hand.

"Move, Ques!" Cherry yelled as she tried shoving him from

her path.

"You got this one," Anna smiled.

"Bitch, I got this one the next one and I'm gonna have the one after that. Fuck is you talkin' about?" Cherry huffed.

"We'll be seeing a lot of each other," Anna assured as she walked around Jacques out the front door. Cherry grabbed a fist full of her hair before she could get a clean get away yanking her back. "I see its games you like to play. Know that I don't play well with others," she whispered in her ear before shoving her out the front door.

"Neither do I but you're gonna learn soon enough how well I don't play with others either," Anna winked as she turned on her heels to walk away.

Cherry quickly turned to look at Ques with fire in her eyes. "So you're back at it, huh?" She asked slamming the door shut before walking away.

"Back at what?" Ques asked following closely behind her.

"Jacques, what the fuck was that bitch doin' in my house?" Cherry turned to face him once again. She was so pissed she couldn't stop herself from pacing.

I woke up to find the bitch standing in the middle of our bedroom with a tray of breakfast. I don't know how she got in here.

"Who is she?" Cherry asked with both hands on her hips.

"She's a chick I use to mess around with way back in the day," he answered.

"How long have this been goin' on? Don't think about lying either," she said with a finger in his face.

"Over a year, at first it started out with her calling my phone," he answered truthfully. "I don't know how she got my number or how she knows where we live. Cherry, the bitch crazy," he said.

"Tuh, that hoe haven't seen crazy yet. Jacques a fuckin' year and you're just now tellin' me?" She asked shaking her head.

"I didn't think things were gonna go this far," he said.

"Daddy, you in trouble," Jewel giggled pointing at Jacques before running off.

Both Cherry and Jacques laughed.

"I see you weren't thinking at all. I should have just killed the bitch," Cherry paced once again. "Get rid of that hoe, now." Cherry said storming off.

*

Anna sat in her car looking at her face. Cherry had fucked her lip up. *"She hit hard."* She thought. Cherry had drawn first blood and the games were finally underway. Anna wasn't expecting to come face to face with Cherry so soon but it was what it was. Now she had to move differently. Opening the car door, Anna popped the trunk in search of something heavy. She smiled when she came across a metal baseball bat. "This will do just fine," she mumbled as she tapped it against her hand. She looked both ways before crossing the street. Anna ran her hand across Cherry's pink Benz before swinging the bat connected with it. The bat hit its mark putting a dent into it. Anna didn't stop as she walked around the car swinging the bat breaking the back window out. She didn't stop until the car was full of dents and all the windows were broken.

*

"Mommy!" JJ called as he stood at the window watching Anna mess up her car. "MOMMY!" JJ called out again.

"What's the matter?" Cherry asked as she walked into the room. JJ pointed out the window as he continued to watch Anna ruin his mother car. Cherry rushed over to see what he was talking about.

"No the fuck this bitch didn't. JACQUES!" Cherry screamed as she ran to the door.

Cherry stormed out the door with rage building inside of her.

"Oooohhh daddy really in trouble now," Jewel giggled.

"I told you I don't play well with others," Anna said pointing the bat at Cherry.

"I guess that makes two of us," Cherry spat charging at her. Anna tried to swing the bat but it was too late. Cherry was already tending to that ass. Cherry grabbed the bat yanking Anna her way causing the bat to fly out of her hand. The cat fight was underway. Anna swung but her hits were nothing compared to what Cherry was doing to her. Cherry punched Anna so hard that she lost her footing but never hit the ground only because Cherry was holding her up by her hair. "I told you this wasn't what you wanted," Cherry huffed swinging Anna around as if she was a rag doll. Finally Cherry released her hair and Anna fell to the ground with a thump. Cherry knew something had to be wrong with the bitch because she was smiling, bloody mouth and all.

Cherry didn't need the bat but she grabbed it from the ground. "I'm getting ready to show you how to use a fuckin' bat," she spat holding it over her head. She went to swing it be it stopped in mid-air.

"Chill out," Jacques said catching it in mid-air. Cherry looked at him. "Look, ya fuckin' kids are watching you," he gritted pointing behind him. If they were somewhere different and his kids wasn't watching he would have let Cherry beat the shit out of Anna with that bat all night if she wanted too.

"You know what Ques? I'm too grand for this shit. You want him bitch there he go," Cherry said releasing the bat walking off. "I have more pressing matters to worry about than dealing with this bullshit." Cherry said as she grabbed her babies' hands walking them back inside closing the door behind them.

"Anna, this is my last warning, get ghost because this is one battle you will not win," Jacques said standing over her. "You've been warmed." He said walking away.

*

Cherry was pissed. She had been over the bullshit and wanted nothing more to live her life. She was on the verge of opening her first business. She didn't need any distractions. She had left the game alone a long time ago. She wasn't trying to go back there but if she had too she didn't have a problem doing just that. "*Mothafuckas always tryna make me step out of character."* She thought as she packed her a few things.

"Mommy, where are you going?" JJ asked standing by the door watching Cherry throw clothes into her suitcase. "We are goin' on a little vacation," she answered.

"Is daddy coming too?"

"No, it's just gonna be you, Jewel, and I, okay?" JJ nodded his   head.
Cherry felt like crying she never wanted her babies to see her act out or get into any type of physical altercation but they had.

"Lil' man go play while I talk to mommy," Jacque said walking into the room. He watched as JJ walked out leaving him and Cherry alone.

"Where you think you goin'? Jacques asked looking at Cherry.

She stopped packing to look at him. "I don't think, I know I'm leaving," she said.

"You're ready to pack up and leave me over this bullshit?" He asked. "Cherry, we've been through worst shit than this."

"Jacques, that's just it. I thought we left the bullshit back in New York. I shouldn't have to worry about if *my* man is out fuckin' another bitch nor should I have to worry about crazy ex's that doesn't know what no means," Cherry spat. "Ques we have kids and I have to protect them at all cost."

"Cherry you don't ever have to worry about me stepping out on you. And you don't think I know that? I don't know what she wants-"

"Oh so now you stupid? You don't know what she wants?" Cherry asked cutting him off.

"Fuck her it's about you, me, and our kids," Ques said closing the space between them.

"Jacques, don't touch me. That's ya problem you always thinking with the wrong head," Cherry said pushing him away.

"Can I get a kiss?" He asked grabbing her pulling her into his chest.

"No, nigga move," Cherry said not feeling him to tough. Ques grabbed her face kissing her lips. Cherry kissed him back before biting his bottom lip.

"Ouch, the fuck you do that for?" He asked holding his lip.

"I told you not to touch me," Cherry laughed. Jacques sucked his teeth as he smacked her on the ass.

"You mind as well put that shit up cause you ain't goin' nowhere," he said going to check his lip out in the mirror.

"Mommy, I'm ready to go," Jewel said running into the room. "Are we going to see auntie Nae again? No, I wanna go see Auntie Ray or Brandi, or auntie Dani. Matter fact; tell auntie Vonne or Nija to come get me. I wanna go with them." Jewel said in one breath.

"Princess, you aren't goin' anywhere today," Jacques said coming out of the bathroom.

"Aww man," she pouted folding her arms across her chest.

"What you don't wanna stay here with, daddy?" Jacques asked picking her up. She shook her head no.

"Daddy, I'm always here with you," she said. "I never get to see my aunties anymore." Jewel said.

"Jewel, go get your brother while I talk to mommy," Jacques said putting her down.

Jewel did as she was told, skipping out of the room to see what JJ was doing.

"Cherry, running isn't goin' to solve this problem," Jacques said. Cherry cocked her head to the side.

"Nigga, I'm not running and I know that," Cherry said.

"So why are you packing?"

"I just wanna get away to wrap my head around this. Jacques, you have a crazy ex who I'm sure is willing to do anything to take me out of the picture," answered Cherry. "The crazy thing is I'm not worried about what she wants to do to me. I'm worried about my fuckin' kids." She finished.

"Cherry, we can take the kids to my mom if that's what you wanna do but I need you by my side on this one," Jacques said.

"We shouldn't have to take our kids from the comfort of their own home because you have a bitch that doesn't know what no means," Cherry spat. The more she thought about it the more pissed off she became.

"We don't. I said if you wanted to take them to my mother than we could," Jacques spat matching her attitude.

"Jacques, all I'm goin' to say is, handle this problem once and for all," Cherry said walking out the room to find her babies.

Jacques sighed deeply as he stood there looking around the room. He knew he had to handle this before he lost Cherry over a bitch he didn't want anything to do with. Cherry had proved herself a long time ago. Jacques knew she would always be the only woman he needed in his life and by his side. She made things seem easy when they were really complicated. "Damn, I love that woman," he mumbled to himself. He grabbed his phone to make a phone call.

"What's up?" The caller asked when he answered the phone.

"You busy?" Jacques asked.

"Nah, what's good?" Ink asked.

Ink was a guy who Jacques had met a few years back. He was a tattoo artist and was nice at what he did.

"I need you to fly out. I'm tryna finally get that tattoo we were talkin' about," Jacques said.

"I'm already in Atlanta, just text me your address and I'll be there as soon as I finish with what I'm doin'," Ink said.

"Now that's love. I'm gonna text you. I'll see you when you get here," Jacques said disconnecting the call. He texted Ink his address before leaving his bedroom in search of his kids and lady.

Jacques searched the entire house to find that Cherry and his babies were gone. He was pissed at the fact that she had just walked out on him and didn't explain why. He dialed her number only to get her voicemail. "Fuck!" He said as he took a seat on the couch.

"I can't believe this shit," he mumbled.

Jacques sat in the same spot for over an hour redialing Cherry's cell phone. He still didn't get an answer. The knock at the door caused him to jump to his feet. He snatched the door open ready to go in on Cherry ass only to find, Ink, standing there.

"Damn, you look pissed," Ink said.

"What's good?" Jacques asked pissed that it wasn't Cherry.

"That's because I am," answered Jacques as he stepped to the side letting Ink inside.

"About? If you don't mind me asking," Ink said.

"My lady just walked out with my fuckin' babies," answered Jacques.

"Damn," Ink said as he sat his things on the coffee table. "Are you still getting the tattoo?" He asked.

"Yeah man," Jacques asked removing his shirt.

"A'ight, let me get my shit together. Roll something up," Ink said as he got his tools ready while Jacques rolled a few blunts.

After smoking two L's, Ink started on Jacques tattoo. An hour and a half later he was finished.

"What you think?" Ink asked as Jacques admired the tattoo sitting over his heart. It was a tattoo of Cherry.

Jacques smiled. Ink had done his damn thing like he knew he would.

"This shit go, bruh," Jacques smiled. "How much do I owe you?" Jacques asked going into his pocket.

"This one is on me. I told you that already," Ink said. Thanks to Jacques, Ink, clientele had gone thru the roof. Jacques had introduced him to a lot of heavy weight people in the music business a few years ago. And because of that, he was well known around the world. Traveling coast to coast doing tattoos.

"Nigga, this is how you make ya money," Jacques said.

"Yeah, and thanks to you, I'm traveling worldwide making plenty of money," Ink said. "So this is the least I can do." He said.

"Good lookin' out," Jacques said as he continued admiring his new tattoo.

"You got my math, hit me up whenever," Ink said as he gathered his things to leave.

"You already know," Jacques said dapping Ink up as he walked him to the door.

Now that he had gotten his tattoo, he needed to put his mind on finding where the fuck Cherry had gone with his kids. Jacques rolled another blunt as he dialed Cherry's cell again. He still didn't get an answer, pissing him off that much more.

Before Jacques could roll his blunt he heard the door being unlocked. He got up rushing to the door. Before Cherry could open the door he was opening it for her. "Where the fuck you been?" He asked.

"Jacques, can you at least grab either Jewel or JJ," Cherry said rolling her eyes. She had carried both Jewel and JJ from the car. They had fallen asleep on the way home from the movies.

Jacques grabbed both of them from her carrying them to their room. He undressed them before covering them up, turning the lights out and leaving the room.

Jacques was about to walk pass his room until he saw Cherry standing there undressing. He stepped inside just staring at her. He snapped out of his daze quickly.

"Where were you?" He asked. "I've been blowing ya phone up all day."

"Jacques, I took my babies out to the movies and to eat. Is that okay with you?" Cherry asked walking into the bathroom to take a shower before she laid down. She was tired and very much annoyed.

"You couldn't let me know that's what you were doin'?" He said following her into the bathroom.

"I didn't know I had to tell you I was taken my babies out," Cherry said rolling her eyes.

"You could have told me something. I thought you up and left me taking my fuckin' kids with you," Jacques spat.

"Jacques, please believe if I ever decided to leave you that I will let you know," Cherry said. "I would never take your kids away from you for any reason. They have nothing to do with what we go through." She said turning the shower on checking the temperature of the water.

"Why weren't you answering your phone?" He asked leaning against the sink.

"Really? Are we about to have this conversation while I'm trying to wash my ass?" Cherry asked stepping into the shower.

"Really we are," he said folding his arms across his chest.

"I didn't answer my phone because I cut it off before we went into the movie theaters and I haven't turned it back on yet," Cherry answered. "Are you happy now? Can I take my shower?" She asked.

"What's with the attitude? Are you mad at me about something?" He asked tryna figure out where her attitude was coming from.

"Yes I piss the fuck off!" Cherry answered.

"For what? I'm not cheating on you," Jacques said.

"I'm pissed at the fact that I come home and there's a bitch in my home. Your ex bitch at that. I'm pissed at the fact that you have been keeping it from me for over a fuckin' year. I'm pissed at the fact that I now have to worry about if the bitch is planning on harming my fuckin' kids because she wants you. So there you have it," Cherry said as she slid the glass door to the shower closed.

"And you ain't never gotta cheat on me, baby. If you feel this relationship isn't working out for you, please feel free to let me know so that I can go about my business," Cherry said.

Jacques walked out of the bathroom. He wasn't trying to argue with Cherry. He understood completely where she was coming from and why she felt the way she felt. Because he would feel the same way if the roles were reversed.

Chapter Eight

Ray opened Nae's room door to find her still sleep buried under the covers. "Oh no, get ya ass up," Ray said walking into the room.

"What time is it?" Nae asked from under the covers.

"Time for you to get up," Ray said standing over the bed. "Nae, you have been here for the past two day's coupe up in this room. You aren't gonna get over Kash like this." Ray said pulling the covers off her.

"Fuck Kash," Nae spat.

"Fuck him," Ray shrugged her shoulders. "Come on, Nae. Get ya ass up and dressed. Dani, Brandi, Vonne, and Nija are on their way," Ray informed her. Nae perked up a little she loved spending time with her girls.

"Is it safe to say welcome back to the old Nae?" Ray smiled. She loved the old Nae. The one who didn't give a fuck about anything and did as she pleased. The one who didn't need a nigga for anything. The one who was all about getting money. Ray knew Nae was just in her feelings. She had done the one thing they all said they wouldn't do. Fall in love with a nigga. But they all had fell in love.

"Yes, the bitch is back," Nae laughed.

"Finally!" Ray laughed too.

Lanaya and Keikeo came to Nae's mind. She always worried about her kids. She didn't trust to many people with her babies but she knew they were in good hands. They were with their father; she knew he would die before he let anything happen to them.

Kash had been blowing her phone up for the past two days but she refuse to answer or talk to him. Moving on wasn't gonna be easy but she felt it was something she had to do. Kash was the only nigga in the streets wild enough to tame her and captured her heart inexpertly. Nae wasn't sure if the love they had for each other was strong enough to keep them together this go round.

"What's the plan?" Nae asked as she got out of bed walking to the bathroom.

"You know I love them damn strippers. I got a few locked in my phone who doesn't mind coming to show us a good time," Ray smiled.

"And I got a pocket full of ones I don't mind sliding in their G-strings," Nae laughed.

"Aye, it's a party!" Ray said leaving Nae to get dress.

*

Melo sat in the middle of the couch with a blunt between his lips and his phone glued to his ear.

"Fuck y'all niggas, been up too?" He asked. He was on a conference call with his niggas King, Chase, Jacques, Jason, Rell, and Kash.

"You already know we still out here getting this money," Rell said referring to him and Jason. They were the only two who decided to stay in New York. They were New York niggas to the heart and that would never change.

"Y'all lil' niggas need to leave New York alone," Chase said.

"Fuck I look like leaving my home?" Jason asked. "I'm gonna be here to the day I die."

"Word," Rell agreed.

"Why this bitch Anna showed up to my crib," Jacques said. "I woke up to find this bitch standing over me with a tray of food."

"What?" They all asked at the same time.

He went on to replay the entire ordeal to his niggas not leaving a damn thing out.

"Wow!" Chase said.

"You should have put a bullet in that bitch dome," King said.

"I see ya ass didn't learn the first time," Melo said.

"I wanted too but my kids was there," Jacques said,

"Ayo, Kash fuck you so quiet for?" King asked his older brother.

"Just thinking that's all," answered Kash.

"You feel like filling us in?" Melo asked.

"Things over here are all bad," Kash sighed.

"Explain, you know these niggas slow as fuck," Jacques laughed.

"Nigga fuck you!" They all laughed.

Kash filled them in on the events of his life.

"Y'all niggas can't win for losing," Chase said.

"What Cherry and I have is Gangsta Luv 'til death do us part," Ques said. "We've weathered one storm I'm sure we can weather this one."

"Man, Nae ass done. I did what I said I would never do and that was hurt her. I fucked another bitch all because she was blackmailing me. It only made my situation worst turning my world upside down." Kash said.

"Kash, Nae stubborn as hell but she loves you." Rell said.

"You better fight because you will never find another chick like her." King said.

"Word, none of us will," Jason said.

"I can say we lucked the fuck up." Chase said.

"We got one of kind bitches," Melo said.

"Who are you callin' a bitch, nigga?" Ray asked walking into the room. "Get ya feet off my coffee table. What I tell you about that?" They heard her ask. They laughed because they knew Ray was the craziest out of all their ladies. She would shoot a nigga and tell him he bet not bleed.

"Ma, I'm the king of this castle," Melo said leaning up smacking Ray on her ass as she walked by.

"Stop play," she said throwing a pillow at him.

"Kash you need us to fly down there?" Rell asked always ready to put in work.

"Nah, I'm not involving any of you niggas. We left the game alone for a reason. I won't have y'all niggas putting y'all life on the line for my fuck ups," answered Kash. "This is something I gotta do on my own."

"Kash you know Nae out here right?" Melo asked.

Slap!

"Ma, watch that shit. Fuck you hit like that for?" Melo asked rubbing the back of his head.

"Why you running ya mouth like a bitch?" Ray asked. "If she wanted him to know where she was she would have told him."

"You have no more times to hit me," Melo warned pissed. His niggas were too weak.

"Shut up, you ain't gonna do shit." Ray said.

Melo walked around grabbing Ray throwing her back against the wall.

"Fuck I tell you about putting ya hands on me?" He whispered in her ear as he wrapped his hand around her neck squeezing lightly before applying a little more pressure. "Stop playing with me, ma before I fuck you up," he said kissing her lips before letting her go.

"Eww get a room," Nae said entering the room.

"First off we are in a room, thank you," Melo said walking away. "Nae, Kash wanna holla at you," he said holding his phone out for her.

"Fuck you and Kash," Nae spat flipping him off. She was

pissed that Melo had gave her up.

"Nae don't even sweat that. We about to get his ass back for opening his mouth," Ray said walking to answer the door. *"Right on time."* She thought opening the door to find Cherry and Jewel standing there.

"Hi Auntie Ray," Jewel said hugging her.

"What are you doin' here?" Ray asked Cherry.

"I needed to get away before I lost my cool and Jewel wanted to see her auntie," Cherry answered as she stepped into the house.

"Trouble in paradise for you too, huh?" Ray asked. Cherry nodded her head yes. "I should have known that's the only time I get to see you bitches."

"That isn't true. Between tryna get my agency open and raising two already grown kids I don't have time for myself," Cherry said.

"Melo, it looks like you're on babysitting duties," Ray said as he walked into the kitchen.

"UNCLE!" Jewel screamed running to him. He picked her up spinning her in the air.

"What's up lil' ma?" He asked.

"Now we gotta move the party to the club, even better," Ray said looking at Jewel.

"What party?" Cherry asked.

"Bitch, what are you doin' here?" Nae asked walking into the kitchen when she saw Cherry.

"Drama, my life story," Cherry answered as they hugged.

"You too, huh?" Nae asked. "Jewel, give me a hug," she said reaching for Jewel.

Jewel shook her head no as she wrapped her little arms around Melo's neck holding on for dear life.

"Her and Lanaya gonna make me kick their little asses," Nae laughed.

"Vonne has finally arrived," Vonne said as she entered the kitchen holding her hands in the air.

"Bitch," Brandi laughed walking in behind her along with Dani and Nija.

"Auntie Vonne!" Jewel screamed reaching out for Vonne.

"Oh lord hell has just frozen over," Vonne laughed as she took Jewel from Melo. Everyone laughed. "Y'all know I'm serious, kids and I don't mix like water and oil."

"Ray, where them strippers you were tellin' us about?" Brandi asked.

"Right, I came prepared," Dani said going into her purse pulling out rubber bands filled with ones.

"What strippers?" Melo asked looking around the room. "Ray, don't get fucked up.

Vonne put Jewel down telling her to go in the next room because the conversation was too much for her little ears.

"Boy bye," Ray waved him off.

"Nigga, ain't you babysitting?" Nija asked. Melo forgot she

was in the room too, she was so damn quiet.

"Oooohhh mommy, uncle smoking those brown cigarettes daddy smoke," Jewel said running back into the kitchen. "Mommy, you know the ones that leave the house smelling funny?" Everyone looked at each other before bursting into a laughing fit.

"Don't be laughing at my baby," Cherry said picking her up.

"I'm sorry but that was too funny," Vonne said still laughing. "She said the brown cigarettes her daddy smoke the ones that leave the house smelling funny." Vonne had tears running from her eyes. Cherry flipped her off. "Girl, those aren't cigarettes." She said still laughing.

Melo grabbed Jewel taking her into the other room with him. "It's gonna be just us two tonight. What you wanna watch?" He asked.

"Dora!" Jewel said.

"Okay, so let's go get dress and bounce. You two can fill us in over some strong drinks while we fill these strippers G-strings," Ray said.

They all got up to leave the kitchen for a ladies night filled with good liquor and good times.

*

They ladies were all dressed up sitting in the males strip club getting drunk while stuffing singles in the strippers G-strings.

"Work that shit, nigga!" Vonne yelled tossing money on the main stage.

They all were feeling good.

"Ray, do they do private shows?" Brandi asked. Ray laughed.

"Yes," she answered.

"Shit, I'm gonna have to get a pole for my room and invite a few of these niggas over for a few private shows," Brandi laughed.

"Chase ain't having that," Dani said. Brandi rolled her eyes.

"Chase ain't gonna know," she said. "I love my nigga but I like to be entertained once in a while."

Nae was tryna have a good time with her girls but her mind has been on Kash and her babies. He had been blowing her up all night but she never answered any of his calls. It got to the point he started texting her.

Nae didn't wanna call or talk to Kash but something was telling her something wasn't right. She excused herself heading to the ladies room. As soon as she stepped inside she whipped out her phone to dial Kash number but he was calling her back.

"What?" She answered with an attitude.

"Fuck that attitude you got. I had to send the kids to New York with Lisa," Kash said with an attitude to match. Nae's heart dropped, she knew it had to be serious if Kash took the kids to stay with Lisa.

"Kash, what happened? Are my babies okay?" Nae nervously asked.

"If you would have answered ya fuckin' phone when I first called you," Kash spat.

"Just answer my fuckin' question!" Nae yelled.

Kash informed her of what happened and why he had to send the kids up north. Nae heart beat loudly in her chest.

"Kash, I'm goin' to kill that bitch," Nae warned as she hung up on him rushing out of the bathroom.

She made it back to her girls with tears in her eyes. Everyone stopped what they were doing as they waited to see if Nae was going to informed them of what was going on.

"I have to go," was all she said as she grabbed her purse rushing out the door.

"NAE!" Cherry called as she chased after her. The rest of the ladies followed. Ray dialed Melo to let him know to get their private jet ready to go.

"What happened?" Nija asked as they caught up to Nae.

"That bitch has got to go," Nae said as she got into the car. Tears were threaten to fall but she refused to let them.

"Who?" Dani asked. Nae hadn't filled them in yet as to why she was in New Orleans.

"Maria," She said as they all piled into the Range Rover.

"Maria?" They asked at once.

"I thought the hoe died years ago?" Vonne said. Nae shook her head no.

"She's gonna wish she had when I get my fuckin' hands on her," Nae warned.

"What happened?" Brandi asked this time.

Nae filled them in as they pulled out of the parking lot. Everyone sober now.

"Ray, I need to get to the airport like yesterday," Nae said as she shook uncontrollably.

"The jet should be ready to go as soon as we pull up to the airport," Ray informed her.

The entire ride was a quiet one as everyone sat lost in their own thoughts.

Nae didn't let the car come to a complete stop before he feet was on the ground. She rushed over to the jet where a tall dark-skin man dressed in a black suit stood waiting to greet her. She didn't have time for small talk she needed to get home so that she could handle this problem once and for all.

"Good evening, I'm-"

"Listen, I don't have time for small talk. I need for you to get this mothafuckin' jet in the air as fast as you can and to LA even faster," she said starting her way up the stairs with her girls right behind her.

*

Kash had returned to Cali the next day after dropping his kids off. It fucked with him that they had to witness what they did. They were young and didn't quite understand what had happened but he was sure they would always remember their home getting raided and torn apart over some bullshit they had no idea of.

He had been calling Nae since it happen and she hadn't answered his calls until a while ago. She had the nerve to answer with a fucking attitude, something he didn't give a fuck about at the moment. He knew she was pissed which was why he didn't chase after her the day she left. He was hoping the time would heal her wounds but things were only getting worst. He had thought about it long and hard on his back up north and back home. Payback was in order.

Kash has spoken to his niggas earlier that day letting them know just how fucked up his life was once again. Shit never seemed to go good for him no matter how hard he tried to stay away from the drama. He reached into his pocket for his phone only to pull out Nae's engagement ring. He looked at it sighing deeply. He was the only nigga wild enough to tame her but now he was wonder was he wild enough to keep her?

Kash replaced the ring in his pocket before dialing Chase up.

"What up, nigga?" Chase answered on the third ring.

"I need for you to get me as much information on Maria as you can," Kash said into the phone. "Oh and a Detective name Ross. I don't know his first name." He finished.

"A'ight, I'll hit you back when I got something," Chase said disconnecting the call.

Kash knew Chase could find any information on anyone; he was just that nice with a computer.

Kash rolled him a blunt filled with loud. He needed something to calm his racing heart.

Lighting his blunt he leaned back thinking about the last two years of his life. For the most part things had been good. He had fucked up by fucking Maria. He regretted it but it was done and there wasn't a damn thing he could do to take it back. Nae had always been enough women for him and there wasn't an excuse for what he had done. She was rough around the edges but he loved her none the less. He smiled as he thought on the day he had laid eyes on her that day in front of Rucker Park. Kash couldn't see himself living without her. But his reality was that he may just lose her for his fucked up ways, he had no one to blame but himself. "Fuck!" He said rubbing the back of his neck.

"Kash!" Nae called out as she stormed into the house. Kash could hear more than one pair of high heels clicking against the floor and knew her girls were with her. "I don't have time for the bullshit," he mumbled standing up.

"Where the fuck is that bitch?" Nae asked storming into the room. Nae didn't give him time to say anything. "You're gonna take me to that bitch right fuckin' now."

"Damn, bruh, get it together," Cherry said shaking her head.

Kash just looked at Nae. The pain she wore on her face let him know just how bad he had hurt her. Something he never wanted to see. "Say something!" Nae snapped as she walked up punching him in his chest. "Kash, I swear you and I are over. That bitch can have you and ya fucked up ways," she spat as she continued punching him in his chest. Kash stood there taking it all. He let Nae take some of her hurt and frustration out on him.

"I'm sorry," was the only thing he could think to say.

"You are sorry. Now take me to that bitch now," she said turning to walk away. She headed upstairs to change into a pair of black sweats and black tank top and a pair of all black Tims.

Nae came back downstairs ready to go. Kash ringing phone stopped any movement that had been going on. Everyone looked at him waiting for him to answer.

"What?" He answered.

"Have you had enough yet?" Maria laughed.

"Bitch you think this shit funny?" Kash asked pissed.

As soon as Nae heard the word bitch she rushed over to Kash snatching his phone from his hands.

"I see you didn't have enough when I cut ya ass up," Nae said heatedly. "You should have stayed gone. But when I get done with you you're gonna wish you had." Maria laughed.

"Thank god for plastic surgery and Kash deep pockets. Oh and tell that nigga I said thanks for the house," Maria said as she continued laughing pissing Nae off.

"You paid for this bitch plastic surgery and brought her a fuckin' house?" Nae asked looking at Kash. He sighed answering her question without opening his mouth. Nae laughed, she was disgusted.

"Bitch, I hope you got insurance," Nae said hanging up.

"Bruh, you down bad for that shit," Cherry said shaking her head.

Kash looked around the room to find all eyes on him. He was surprised Ray had yet to say anything. She was the one who didn't give a fuck how bad you felt about what you did. She was gonna make you feel worst. Hell all them did but her and Vonne was the worst by a long shot.

"Fuck you lookin' at me for?" Ray asked.

"I'm surprised you ain't got shit to say," Kash said.

"Nigga, I didn't fly all the way out here to talk. It's murking season," Ray said.

"Let's go," Nae said walking to the door. Before getting in the car she grabbed a can of gas from the garage. No questions were asked because they already knew what she was gonna do with it.

The entire ride neither her or Kash said anything to each other. Her girls were in two different cars riding closely behind them.

*

"Y'all think Nae really gonna burn this bitch shit down?" Vonne asked with a little chuckle.

Ray looked at her thru the rear-view mirror.

"Bitch, if she burnt that nigga shit down what makes you think she isn't gonna burn hers down?" Cherry asked.

"If she don't I will. I just hope the hoe is inside," Ray said.

"Why y'all think I don't love these niggas?" Vonne asked. "Too much to deal with."

"So what you call with you and Jason has?" Cherry asked.

"A mutual understanding," answered Vonne. Ray laughed.

"Bitch, you love that nigga," Ray said.

"I'm not gonna lie and say I don't because I really do. But, like I said before we have a mutual understanding.

*

"I hope Nae and Kash get thru this too," Nija said.

Brandi and Dani looked at her. "Girl, I hope so too but Kash has fucked up bad," Brandi said.

"This nigga done paid for the bitch plastic surgery and brought her a fuckin' house." Dani said. "His ass should have just walked away. He knows Nae don't play like that.

"Y'all think he fucked her?" Nija asked. Brandi and Dani looked at each other.

"Hell yeah," they answered at the same time.

"Why, is what I wanna know," Nija said.

"That's something we are all wondering," Dani said. Brandi agreed as they came to a complete stop.

*

"This is where this bitch lives?" Nae asked Kash finally saying anything to him. He nodded his head up and down. "You really brought this?" Once again Kash nodded his head up and down. Nae shook her head in disgust before getting out of the car.

Nae slammed the door behind her as she walked up to the front door. She banged on the door as she called for Maria.

"Bitch, didn't I tell you I was coming to burn ya shit down?" Nae asked banging on the door. "Open the fuckin' door!" She yelled now kicking on the door.

"Kash, open the door. I know you have a key," Nae said turning to face him.

Kash reached into his pocket tossing the keys to Nae. Nae caught them. She let herself in and searched the place. He girls followed her inside. While Kash stood outside shaking his head. Nae came across a picture of Maria and Kash. Snatching it up she threw it on the floor breaking the glass frame it was in.

"This shit nice," Vonne said as everyone looked at her. "What?" She asked.

No one said anything as they walked around trashing the place.

"KASH!" Nae called out.

He walked in looking around. "Call that bitch I have a few words for that hoe," Nae said waiting for him to dial Maria's number. Kash did as he was told handing Nae the phone.

"Papi, I see you finally came to your senses," Maria purred into the phone. Nae laughed.

"No bitch he didn't. It's one thing to fuck with me but you drew the line by involving my kids," Nae said into the phone.

"Oh it's you," Maria laughed.

"Yes, it's me. I hope you enjoyed this little house cause it's about to go up in flames," Nae laughed before hanging up. She threw Kash his phone as she started pouring gas all around the place. Fishing in her pocket for a light Nae found one flicking it on as she removed a blunt from her pocket. She inhaled the smoke before tossing the blunt into the gas. Everyone watched as the flames went up.

Chapter Nine

Melo woke up to find Jewel passed out beside him on the couch. *"Finally."* He thought as he picked her up carrying her off to bed. Jewel had been with him for the past two days wearing him out. One minute she wanted to play Barbie's, next she wanted to watch Dora, than she wanted to have a tea party and whatever they didn't have he was driving her to Toys R Us to get them leaving the store spending more than he had planned. To top things off he hadn't spoken to any of the girls since they had left.

"Ray talkin' bout she want a girl. Hell no," Melo mumbled as he laid Jewel in the bed. He tucked her in before leaving the room. On his way to his bedroom he by passed a mirror and stopped. "Come on, really Jewel?" He asked staring at his reflection. She had put pink lipstick on his lips and some of his dreads were in ponytail holders. Melo sighed as he covered his face with his tatted hands only to be surprised once again. *"They are coming to get her ass today."* He thought walking off in search of his cell phone.

Melo searched for his cell and his brown cigarette as Jewel liked to call it. He located his phone dialing Jacques.

"Yo?" Jacques answered.

"Son, come get ya daughter," Melo said dead serious. Jacques laughed.

"What she do?"

"She got me spending money on everything, twice at that. Then I wake up to find my face painted on like I'm a fuckin' coloring book and my finger nails painted pink!" Melo yelled into the phone. Ques was weak.

"Nigga, you need the practice. Didn't you say Ray wanted a little girl?"

"Fuck all that her little ass is very persuasive. I have been to Toys R Us about four times in the past two days. I done brought her little ass shoes and clothes, I done been a damn horse and I done sipped on fake tea," Melo laughed.

"Nigga, welcome to parenthood, that's the life of a father," Ques said. "What is my lil' ma up to anyways?"

"She's sleep finally," answered Melo.

"You gonna have to meet me in New York with her. I'm taking the kids to my mom for a while," Jacques said.

"Why what's up?" Melo asked.

"Until I can get this shit with Anna under control," Jacques said.

Melo shook his head. He didn't understand how Kash and Ques stayed in the middle of bullshit. It was as if they relationship was tainted.

*

Kash sat in the basement with the lights out listening to the radio. They were jamming with slow jams. He bopped his head to the music as Differences by Ginuwine spilled from the speakers. He had a drink in one hand and a blunt sitting between his full lips.

He knew if he didn't do something fast, he would lose the

love of his life and his family.

"I may have already lost, Nae." He thought. Kash sighed as he ran his hands over his face. He had never wanted anyone as badly as he wanted Nae. He was the one to blame for the fuck up and once again he found himself tryna fix something that should have never been broken. Kash got up in search of Nae. Since she had burned Maria's home down they hadn't seen much of each other. Nae kept her distances as best she could.

Kash finished off his drink as he stood there thinking about the conversation he and Brandi had the day before.

Kash sat in the kitchen nursing yet another drink when Brandi walked in finding him with the puppy dog face on. She laughed as she shook her head.

"Nigga, shake this shit off and prove to her that she's who you want," she said as she grabbed a bottle of water.

Kash sighed.

"I fucked up. I don't know if we can come back from this one."

Brandi sucked her teeth and rolled her eyes. "We all know you fucked up but moping around isn't gonna win her back. Kash, ya ass better do something before you find the love of ya life in the arms of another man," Brandi said. "Listen, we all know how stubborn and bullheaded Nae can be but that's how she protects herself from getting hurt. Think about this. If it was really over do you think she would have burnt that house down?" Kash looked at Brandi as he thought about the question.

"Yeah," they both said at the same time sharing a laugh.

"True, would she still be here if it was really over? The kids aren't here. Which means she doesn't have any real reason to be here," Brandi said.

"Gaining her trust back is goin' to be hard to do," Kash sighed.

"It is but as long as you gain it back. Yes it's goin' to take some time but you two have been thru enough to weather this storm." Brandi said. "You and Nae are meant for each other. I'm rooting for the two of you." Brandi said patting Kash on his back.

"Thanks for the talk, B," Kash said getting up to give her a hug.

"No thanks needed. Just get ya shit together," Brandi said walking away.

Kash shook his thoughts as he left his fully furnished basement to find Nae.

*

Nae stood in front of her full length mirror admiring her frame. Despite having twins Nae body was still on point. The way her ass sat up in her Seven jeans would have niggas taking a second look. She was single again.

"Bitch, fuck you goin'?" Vonne asked as she laid across Nae's bed.

"She isn't goin' anywhere," Kash said walking into the room. Both Vonne and Nae rolled their eyes.

"I'll be getting ready," Vonne said as she got off the bed leaving the room so that they could talk.

"We'll see," Nae said looking herself over once again.

"We need to talk," Kash said taking a seat admiring just how beautiful Nae was.

"I don't have anything to talk to you about," Nae said as she grabbed the six inch over the knee Michael Kors boots.

"Nae, I didn't mean to hurt you. That's something I never intended to do...."

"But you did," Nae spat cutting him off.

"And I'm sorry for that. I love you. I thought I was doin' what I had to do to keep you from harm's way," Kash said.

"You thought by fuckin' the next bitch was keeping me out of harm's way?" Nae asked laughing. "Look where thinking like that got you."

"Nae, what the fuck was I supposed to do. She was blackmailing me?!" Kash yelled jumping to his feet.

"Tell me!" She yelled back. "But no you kept it goin' for over a year. How can she blackmail you for something I've done?" She asked on the verge of crying.

Kash sighed running his hands over his waves and face.

"Kash, I love you but this was the icing on the cake. I don't think I can forgive you for this one," Nae said turning her back to him so that he couldn't see the tears forming in her eyes.

"You don't mean that," Kash said walking up behind her

wrapping his arms around her holding her close. Nae damn near melted in his arms. She would miss his strong arms wrapped around her but leaving him was something she had to do. She felt it wasn't fair that she had to keep fighting over someone who belonged to her. He had always made her feel safe and secure, but now all she felt was pain and hurt something she never wanted to feel or endure. Here they both were standing in between her and Kash.

"Kash, I do. I love you but I think this is best for the both of us," Nae said turning to face him not caring about the tears running down her face.

Kash used his thumbs to wipe the tears away. Seeing Nae cry was something Kash hated, especially if he was the reason. Kash held her face in his palms staring into her face. "I love you 'til death do us part," Kash whispered. "I'm gonna give you your space but I'm not giving up on us. I will never give up on us." He assured kissing her lips softly.

Nae kissed him back before pulling away. She ran into the bathroom slamming the door behind her, locking herself in it.

Kash stood at the door listening to her cry. Shit broke his heart, but he was gonna do everything in his power to win her back. It didn't matter what it took. He knew he needed her just as bad as he need air to breathe, his heart wouldn't accept the fact the nothing or no one else. They belonged together.

"I'm goin' to win you back. I promise that, ma," Kash whispered before walking off.

*

Nae didn't know how many times she said she wouldn't cry over or for Kash anymore but how could she not? She loved him to death. They made each other stronger. They had a love that was supposed to be unbreakable. He had broken his promise, when he said he would never break her heart.

Nae cleaned her face going on about her night. She knew clubbing wasn't going to solve any of her problems but that would be her escape for now. This was a reality she didn't want to deal with. Nae finished up in the bathroom before she went to search for her girls.

She bumped into Cherry on her way out here room. "Where are you goin'? Nae asked.

"Girl, here I am all the way in Cali as if I don't have my own bullshit to deal with back at home," Cherry answered. "Running from my problems isn't gonna solve them. So I'm on my way home to deal with 'em head on." she finished.

"You're not gonna stay to go out with me?" Nae asked pouting.

"Not this time. Nae you need to deal with the issues you and Kash have. You love that nigga, work it out," Cherry said. "We've been through worst shit than this. This is yet another road block in our path to happiness."

"Cherry, he fucked my heart up with this one," Nae said.

"I understand that but is it enough to throw away what you two have built already?"

"He did it once, what makes you think he won't do it again

if another bitch starts blackmailing him?" Nae wanted to know.

"Hopefully there isn't gonna be a next time. Because he knows what's on the line," answered Cherry. "You know whatever you do, I have ya back." She said hugging Nae.

"I know," Nae smiled as they shared a sisterly hug. "I love you, bitch."

Cherry laughed, "I love you too."

They two headed downstairs. "Wait all of y'all are leaving?" Nae asked seeing her girls dressed and ready to go.

"I gotta get home to my baby," Ray said. "You already know I'm only a phone call away."

"Aww, I wanted to go out," Nae pouted once again.

"We gonna have to take a rain check," Dani said.

"Word, Chase been blowing me up tryna go in on my shit," Brandi laughed. "He done got wind of them pictures from the other night in the strip club. He's pissed so there for I have to go make it up to him."

"Ewwww!" Nae said. Everyone laughed.

"You'll be alright," Brandi continued to laugh.

"That's probably what this bitch needs. Some dick," Vonne said.

Nae rolled her eyes. "Dani and Nija, are y'all leaving too?" Nae asked.

They both nodded their heads. "Y'all asses are cold for that," Nae said flopping on the couch.

"Bitch, you need to be working it out with Kash," Brandi said. Nae rolled her eyes.

"Handle ya business," Ray said as they all got ready to go.

Nae watched as her girls left wondering what she was going to do now. She snatched her phone up to dial Kendra.

"Oh bitch you remembered my number?" Kendra answered her phone. Nae laughed.

"Girl, you don't know that half," Nae said. "How about I fill you in over a few drinks?"

"You know I'm always down for a party," answered Kendra.

"Good, I'll meet you at Uptowns in a half," Nae said disconnecting the call.

*

The entire plane ride home Cherry thought about both her and Nae's situations. She knew that she wasn't giving up on Jacques that easy. She had invested too much time into their relationship to give up on it. She knew Nae felt the same way but was just hurting. Cherry didn't know when all the bullshit would leave them alone and let them be happy. She just prayed it would be soon. As she drove home from the airport she dialed Melo to check on Jewel. She knew her baby girl was in good hands but she hadn't spoken to neither of them in two days. Two days to long.

"Fuck you want?" Melo answered his phone.

"Nigga, where's my baby?" Cherry asked.

"Up top with Lisa," he answered.

"What, why?" Cherry asked.

"I don't know. Jacques asked me to fly her up there so I did," he answered.

"Was my baby good?" Cherry asked laughing.

"She was a little princess," Melo spat sarcastically.

"Fuck you, Melo!" Cherry laughed.

"Nah, but you gonna have to bring her and JJ down more often. I enjoyed her company, with her spoiled ass," he laughed.

"You don't have to tell me that but once. So when do you want them?" Cherry laughed.

"Whenever," he answered.

"Don't be surprised if I'm dropping them off next week," Cherry said.

"That won't be a problem," Melo assured.

"Thanks Melo," Cherry said before disconnecting the call. Cherry shook her head because Melo and the rest of his niggas had Jewel and Lanaya spoiled as hell. It was as if none of them knew how to say no to a three and two year old.

*

Anna walked around Jacques and Cherry's home as if she belonged there. The place was lovely. She continued to walk around admiring the paint job pictures of their family hanging all around the house and frowned. *"I'm supposed to be that bitch in those pictures."* She thought making her way upstairs. She walked into their bedroom turning the lights on. Anna stripped out of her clothes before climbing into the king size bed. She ran her hands around the silky sheets before letting her body sink deeper into the bed. She moaned closing her eyes thinking about Jacques. Before Anna knew it her hands were sliding down her body. Anna stopped quickly removing her hands. She didn't wanna play with herself that's what she had Jacques for. She rolled on her stomach giggling. She slipped from the bed walking over to the closet. It was his and her walk-in closet. One side was Cherry's and the other's Jacques. "This bitch has good taste," Anna mumbled as she skimmed thru Cherry's clothes. Some still had tags on them. She turned to Ques things inhaling his scent as she wrapped her arms around a few of his clothes. "You smell so good, daddy," she whispered removing one of his button up shirts from the hanger. She placed it around her before walking back into the bedroom. She climbed back into the middle of the bed rolling around in his shirt with a smiled glued to her face.

*

Cherry and Jacques pulled up to the house at the same time. He got out first.

"Didn't I tell you that you weren't goin' anywhere?" He asked opening the door for her. Cherry rolled her eyes.

"Nigga, you are not my father," she spat.

"Cherry running from our problems isn't gonna solve shit," Jacques said.

"I know that which is why I came back home," she answered as she let them inside. "Why did you take my babies to New York?" She asked.

"I needed them far away from this bullshit as possible," answered Ques wrapping his arms around Cherry. "I love you," he whispered kissing her ear.

"I love you too," she assured as they made their way upstairs.

Jacques stopped Cherry turning her around to face him, he picked her up carrying her the rest of the way. Their lips locked the rest of the way to the bedroom.

"Hi daddy, I've been waiting all night for you," Anna said stopping their kissing session. Cherry head flipped back to find Anna lying in the middle of her bed wrapped in one of Jacques shirts. Cherry sighed. She knew Anna was always gonna be a problem until one of them was dead.

"Bitch!" Cherry spat as Jacques put her down. "I see that ass whipping didn't teach you anything." Cherry said going after her. Anna laughed as she rolled off the bed before Cherry could grab her.

"I see me fuckin' up that pretty Benz of yours didn't teach you anything," Anna shot back. "Cherry, there's only enough room for one of us, and it isn't you." She said with her hands on her hips.

"Anna, what part don't you understand? I don't want you," he said.

"Baby, you don't believe that yourself. You just need a little push," Anna smiled.

Jacques sighed deeply.

"I'm getting ready to give ya ass a little push," Cherry spat as she walked across the room. She was going to push her ass right out her bedroom window. Anna moved out the way just in time. Cherry had swung just missing her face. Anna could feel the wind and was happy she was quick on her feet. She knew for a fact that she would have been knocked the fuck out!

Jacques grabbed Cherry holding her back.

"Why the fuck are you always grabbing me?" Cherry asked pushing Jacques off her. "I told you to handle this bitch and you didn't."

"I said I was goin' to handle it," Jacques gritted.

"Fuck is you mad at?" Cherry asked. "I should be the only one standing here mad."

"Daddy, if you were with me you wouldn't have to worry about me talkin' to you like that," Anna said. "If you said you would handle something I would let you handle it."

"Bitch," Cherry said as she went after her again. Anna tried to jump on the bed but missed as she lost her footing.

"Aahh shit!" She yelled as she hit the floor hard. Cherry was in rage as she grabbed her legs dragging her across the floor. Anna tried kicking her way out of Cherry's strong grip but she couldn't.

"You know what?" Cherry said as she let Anna go. "I said I

wasn't goin' thru this and that this was something you had to handle," she said looking at Jacques. "As much as I would love to whoop this hoe's ass, I'm not." She said as she walked off. That bitch better be out my house in two minutes," Cherry warned over her shoulders.

Jacques put his attention back on Anna who was smiling from ear to ear.

"I don't see a damn thing funny," he spat very much annoyed. "Anna, I need for you to understand that I don't want you." He said.

"Oh but you do. I'm gonna show you that you wanna be with me," Anna said as she slowly walked over to him. She placed her hand on his chest. Jacques grabbed her forcefully by the back of her neck.

"You know I like it rough," Anna moaned as she was being pulled and dragged from the bedroom.

"Listen," he said as he opened the front door. "Go find someone else to fuck with," he said pushing her out the door. Once again Anna lost her footing and fell face first into the ground. She smiled as she rolled onto her back.

"Jacques, you shouldn't be like that to your future wife," Anna said licking her lips.

"Bitch, you gotta be out ya rabbit ass mind to think some ill shit like that," he said. "This will be the last warning I'll give you," he said closing the door and locking the it.

Jacques sighed deeply as he went and searched for Cherry. He knew she was pissed. How could she not be? When she comes home to find another bitch lying in the middle of her bed. His ex bitch at that.

Jacques found Cherry in the family room with her kindle in her hands.

"There isn't anything to talk about. Just handle that bitch before I do it," Cherry said never looking up from her kindle.

Jacques grabbed the kindle from her hands placing it on the coffee table before he took a seat pulling Cherry on his lap.

"I love you," he said kissing her lips.

"And I love you too. Jacques this shit has gone on long enough," Cherry said.

"I know and I will handle it like I said I would."

"I heard you the first time when you said you were gonna handle it," Cherry said. "Now can I get back to reading?"

"Hell no, the kids are gone and we finally have to house to ourselves. It's about time we do some grown up things," Jacques smiled.

"Nope," Cherry said as she climbed off his lap.

"Fuck you mean no?" He asked. Cherry knew how much he hated hearing the word no, when he wanted some pussy.

"Just what I said, Jacques you are in the dog house," she said.

"In the dog house?" Fuck is that supposed to mean?"

"It means that you can't get any pussy until you handle

that Anna problem," answered Cherry as she grabbed her kindle walking off.

"Are you fuckin' serious?" Jacques asked.

"I'm oh so serious," Cherry answered over her shoulders.

"That's some straight up and down bullshit," Jacques huffed.

Jacques got up in search of some weed. He kept a stash around the house. *"This is gonna be a long ass night."* He thought.

*

Nae and Kendra sat at the bar drinking as Nae caught her up on the bullshit that had been going on in her life.

"Damn sis, that's fucked up," Kendra said. Here she was falling in love and her girl relationship was falling apart. Nae waved her off.

"So what's goin' on with you and your boo?" Kendra smiled.

"We're cool. He treats me well, I'm just scared. I don't wanna put myself out there just to get hurt at the end," Kendra said.

"From what I can tell, Ken, he's really into you," Nae said. "When am I gonna meet him?"

"I'll admit he is. He makes me feel special but that doesn't stop me from being scared," Kendra said. "Shyne is a street nigga with bitches lined up at his front door tryna get in his bed, heart, and pockets."

"Fuck them bitches. If he was checking for any of them he wouldn't be checking for you," Nae said. "At least one of us is happy."

Nae held her hand in the air stopping whatever it was that Kendra was about to say.

"I didn't come here to talk about my problems all night. I came to have a good time to forget about my problems even if it's only for a few hours," Nae said. Kendra nodded her understanding.

"So let's hit the dance floor," Kendra said getting up from her seat.

Uptown was packed from wall to wall.

*

Meccah was in the middle of the dance floor grinding his dick on some random bitch with a cup in his hand and a fat blunt sitting between his full lips.

"Lil' ma got ass on her," he said eyeing Nae as she walked by.

Fuckin' Problem by ASAP Rocky was now spinning. Meccah didn't thank the chick he was dancing with as he walked off leaving her free for the next nigga. He followed Nae and when she found enough room to shake her ass, he stepped behind her pulling her close. Nae didn't bother looking back she didn't give a fuck who she was dancing with. She had gone out to have a good time. Nothing else really mattered.

"Damn," Meccah said as he grabbed her waist. His cologne quickly filled her nose, Nae smiled. "Never met a mothafucka fresh like me/All these mothafuckas wanna dress like me/Put the chrome to your dome make you sweat like Keith/Cause I'm the nigga, the nigga nigga," Meccah rapped in Nae's ear. Nae smiled as she continued dancing on him. She didn't care who she danced with. She just wanted to have a good time to take her mind off the problems she was having at home.

Meccah and Nae danced to a few more songs before she tried walking off.

"Hold up, where you goin'? He asked pulling her back.

"Thanks for the dance, I'm goin' to get me a drink," answered Nae as she finally looked up in his face. *"Damn, he's fine."* She thought taking him in from head to toe.

Meccah had to stand at least 6 foot 3 inches, caramel skin tone, low fade, nice smile, and his gold tee was trimmed to perfection. He was dressed in True's from head to toe with the latest pair of air Jordan's sitting on his feet.

"Can I at least buy you a drink?" He asked not wanting anyone else to grab her attention.

"That you can do," Nae smiled as he wrapped his arm around her shoulder and they walked to the bar.

They both ordered a drink. "What's ya name?" Meccah asked standing between Nae's legs.

She pushed him back. "Nae, but you gonna have to back up a little," she answered.

Meccah laughed, "My bad. I'm Meccah."

"I know a fine ass woman like you isn't single?"

"You're straight forward with ya shit," Nae laughed. "I like that."

"That's the way you gotta be. A nigga to grown to be playing games," Meccah answered handing her the drink the bartender had just sat in front of them. "Thanks!" He said.

"To answer your question, my relationship status is complicated," Nae answered truthfully.

"I can respect that," Meccah said. "I know we just met but maybe we can be friends?" He offered.

"We'll see how that goes," Nae said.

They talked a little while longer. Kendra walked up interrupting their conversation.

Meccah this is Kendra, Kendra, Meccah," Nae said.

"Nice to meet you," Meccah said reaching over to give her a hug.

Kendra stopped him by holding her hand up.

"You friendly aren't you?" She asked. "Anyhow, Nae, I'm sorry to run out on you but my boo wants me home now," Kendra said.

"Really? You just gonna up and leave me?" Nae asked.

"I'm sorry but my baby wants me home," Kendra said. "We can do this again some other time."

"It's cool, I can keep you company," Meccah said joining

the conversation.

Kendra looked at him before she looked at Nae.

"It's cool Kendra, go take care of ya boo," Nae said.

"What about him?" Kendra asked pointing to Meccah.

"What about me?" He asked. "What, I'm not good enough?"

"Kendra, it's cool," Nae laughed seeing the way Kendra was looking at Meccah. "He can keep me company because I'm not ready to home just let."

"A'ight, call me when you get home," Kendra said as she hugged Nae. "And be safe, niggas will do anything for some pussy." Kendra said looking Meccah up and down one last time.

"I will and thanks for coming out with me tonight," Nae said as she watched Kendra walk away.

"What's up, what was that all about?" Meccah asked finally taking a seat on an empty bar stool.

"Ken, just don't trust anybody and she's very over protective of me," answered Nae.

"Shawty was throwing me hella shade and she doesn't even know me," Meccah said.

Nae laughed, "I would tell you to not pay her any mind but you will be a fool if you don't."

When Nae and Meccah wasn't on the dance floor they were stilling at the bar getting to know each other over drinks. Throughout the night he kept her laughing, something she hadn't done in a long time. It felt good but Nae knew her starting a relationship with someone else wasn't what she really wanted to do.

*

"Are you sure you don't want me to drive you home?" Meccah asked as they stood outside of the club.

"I'm sure," Nae said. What the fuck she look like pulling up in the driveway in another niggas car? Knowing her and Kash still lived together.

"Well at least call me when you get home," Meccah said as Nae opened the door to the taxi that had been waiting on her.

"Is that your way of asking for my number?" She asked laughing.

"Something, like that," Meccah laughed too. "Being that you weren't gonna offer it to me."

"Here, put ya number in my phone and I'll do the same," Nae said as she took his cell phone from his hand.

They exchanged numbers before Nae slipped into the backseat of the taxi.

"A'ight, be safe ma," Meccah said closing the door behind her. "And use my number."

"I will, I promise," Nae assured before the cab pulled off.

Nae sat in the back of the taxi wondering if she was wrong for giving another nigga her number knowing she was still in love with Kash. Nae shook the thoughts of Kash and smiled thinking about how much fun she had that night. Nae just wished things could go back the way they use to be with her and Kash. She remembered how they could chill with each other for hours laughing and talking about any and everything. Or how they would sit around watch rap battles on YouTube arguing about who was better. She laughed because they could never agree on that subject, but it was fun none the less.

Before Nae knew it the taxi was coming to a complete stop in front of her home. She paid him before she climbed out of the cab. Before walking up to her front door she removed her phone texting Meccah as she promised to do. Nae let him know that she had made it home safely. She than text Kendra letting her know as well telling her to call her whenever she got up the next day.

Chapter Ten

It had been almost a month since California's finest ran into Kash home violating him and his kids. Kash was on a rampage. They had welcomed him to Cali now it was his turn to welcome them to his world. It had been years since he had killed someone but the rush running thought his body had him amped up. He sat in the living room of the main detective home waiting for him to arrive. Kash knew he lived alone. Kash checked his watch as he waited. He had been sitting there for over an hour and was becoming very impatient, but he knew time was of the essence. *"Finally,"* Kash thought as he heard the front door being unlocked. Kash eased from his seat quickly slipping into the shadows.

Detective Ross had yet another rough day at the office. All he wanted to do was lay back and relax while sipping on a cold beer and a shot of any liquor he could find. If he had any left. Ross removed his coat tossing it on the back of his couch on the way to the bar sitting in the corner of the room. He snatched the bottle of Scotch and a shot glass.

"I'll take a double shot," Kash said coming from his hiding place. Ross went to draw his gun but Kash stopped him. "I wouldn't do that if I was you," he warned showing his .357.

"How did you get in my home?" Ross growled.

"That shouldn't matter too much. As you can see I got in," Kash said.

"What do you want?" Ross asked.

"I wanna know why would you raid my home while my kids were there knowing you wouldn't find a damn thing?"

"I got a tip-"

"You a fuckin' lie!" Kash yelled cutting him off. "What connections do you have with Maria?"

Ross swallowed hard as he thought on what to say. "I'm an officer of the law," Ross said. Kash laughed.

"I don't give a fuck what you are," Kash assured. "You welcomed me to Cali and I'm welcoming you to how I live. Too bad you aren't gonna live long enough to enjoy it." Kash shrugged his shoulders.

"Listen, I can fix this," Ross tried pleading his case. Kash shook his head.

"I'm fixing this problem. Now what connections do you and Maria have?" Kash asked again.

"That's my daughter," Ross finally answered. "Fuck! I told her that wasn't a good idea." He said shaking his head. "She underestimated you," Ross informed Kash.

"Everyone does," Kash said as he pulled the trigger on his .357. He watched as Detective's Ross head exploded like a watermelon. His brain splattered on the wall behind him long before his body hit the ground. Kash stood over his body with a grin on his face. "Welcome to my world." Kash said before turning to leave just as he had come.

Kash walked the few blocks to his car with his head hung low. He hadn't been in the game for the past two years only to move to the west coast to get sucked right back into it. He got into his car starting it up he was getting ready to pull off when his cell rung.

"Hello?"

"Daddy, I wanna come home. Grandma Lisa mean," Lanaya said into the phone. Kash laughed.

"Girl ain't nobody mean, you don't like when someone tell ya bad ass to do something," Lisa said in the background. "She got no more times to roll those damn eyes at me either," she said.

"Daddy, I miss you and mommy," Lanaya said.

"I miss you too baby. I'll be there to get you and Keikeo soon, I promise." Kash said.

"Okay, I love you daddy," she said.

"I love you too, let me talk to grandma," Kash said.

"Hello?" Lisa said getting on the phone.

"You need anything?"

"No, but whatever you and Nae got goin' on I need for y'all to fix it. Kids are involved now," Lisa said into the phone.

"I swear I'm working on it now," Kash assured.

Lisa never got into Kash or Jacques business. She knew it had to be something bad going on for Kash to fly his babies up north.

"Ma, I can't win for losing. If it isn't one thing it's another," Kash sighed.

"Baby, that's just part of life. Nothing is easy. If it's

something you really want you have to work hard for it in order to keep it," she told him. "Kash you have weathered a lot of storms-"

"Well how many more am I gonna have to weather before the storm is over or before it washes me out?" He asked cutting her off.

"No one can answer that but you," she replied. "Nothing in life is easy. Life is what you make of it."

Kash sat quietly listening to Lisa talk. He knew she was right. Over the years she had become the mother him and King didn't have.

"Kamil, things will get better," Lisa said.

"I sure hope so," Kash mumbled. "Ma, call me if you need anything. Thanks again." He said before disconnecting the call. Kash put his mind back on the task at him. Reaching into his pocket he pulled out the piece of paper with the addresses of the officers who raided him home. *"One down."* He thought starting his ride pulling off.

*

Maria had been lying low for almost a month now only because her father had asked her too. She was on a mission and it didn't matter how many times her father told her to walk away she couldn't. Kash did something to her and she wanted to be the one wrapped in his arms every night. She wanted to be the one he woke up to every morning and she wanted to be the one who had his babies. If Maria couldn't have Kash, neither could Nae, her mind was already made up that she would stop at nothing to have Kash in her arms where he belonged.

Maria smiled as she thought about Nae burning her home down. It was a very bold move on her part. She had to give it to Nae, when she came at you she came at you hard. Maria didn't mind it one bit because she would just have Kash buy her a new home, one much bigger for her and his kids. Maria dialed Kash number. She hadn't talked to him or heard his voice in a while.

"Hello?" Kash answered. Maria didn't know what he was doing but she could hear muffing noises in the background.

"Hi papi," she moaned into the phone. Kash sucked his teeth before hanging up on her. She dialed his number right back.

"I advise you to stop callin' my phone and go check on ya dead father," Kash spat into the phone. Maria laughed.

"Kash, my father is just fine. You need not worry about him and worry about me," she said into the phone. Kash chuckled.

"Are you sure about that?" He asked. Maria could hear the seriousness in his voice and knew he had done something to her father.

"Kash, what did you do to my father?" She asked sitting up.

"I did what I should have done to you a long time again," he answered. "I'll killed the mothafucka." At this point Kash didn't give a fuck about anything. He had lost the best thing that ever happened to him, Nae.

"I swear on everything if you killed my father you're gonna

wish you were dead!" She yelled into the phone.

"Maria, fuck off my line. You need to be making funeral arrangements, one," Kash said hanging up.

Maria dialed her father's cell only for it to ring out. She jumped up rushing out the door as her heart pounded away in her chest. She jumped in her car, hoping and praying Kash didn't kill her father.

"This is my entire fault," she mumbled as she drove off. The entire ride to her father's house she dialed his number. "What did I do?" She asked banging her fist into the steering wheel.

Maria's mind was all over the place. She didn't know how she made it to her father's house driving well over the speed limit the entire way there. She parked her car jumping out running to the front door. The door was unlocked so she let herself in.

"Daddy!" She called out. "Daddy, please answer me," she whispered searching his place. She walked in the living room and stopped with wide eyes. There was her father lying in a pool of his own blood. She rushed over to him with eyes filled with tears. "Daddy," she cried as she shook him, his dead eyes staring up at her. Maria broke down even more. He had asked her to leave well enough alone a long time ago but she wouldn't listen.

"Oh daddy, I'm so sorry," she cried on his chest. "Please believe me when I say he will pay for this." She said wiping the tears away. Maria removed her phone and dialed Kash number once again.

"Kash, you took something that meant the world to me

and it's only right I take something that means the world to you," Maria said as soon as Kash answered.

"Maria, fuckin' with you I have already lost everything that meant the world to me," Kash said. Maria laughed.

"You will feel my pain one way or another. The stakes had just been raised," she assured before hanging up on him. Maria than called the police for them to come pick her father's dead body up.

*

Nae had just gotten off the phone with Keikeo and Lanaya. It had been almost a month since she seen her babies. She wanted to go get them but because of what was going on with Maria she rather leave them where they were. She didn't trust Maria and would lose her mind if Maria tried taking her babies. Lanaya and Keikeo were good and she had expected nothing less. What made their little vacation better was that Jewel and JJ was out there with them. Nae missed her babies something awful but she rather be safe than sorry. She couldn't imagine what she would do if anything was to happen to them.

Nae thought about Meccah and smiled. He was a brown skin cutie who dressed nice. He wasn't Kash but he did keep her entertained. They had been talking and texting each other for the past three weeks, he had been trying to convince her to go out on a date with him but Nae kept telling him no. She had told him that she wasn't checking for anything serious, she was just looking to have fun not bothering to go into details of her current situation. Nae couldn't lie she missed Kash. They barely talked or saw each other anymore. If he was home when she decided to come home she would sleep in the kid's room or one of the guest bedrooms. He hadn't been home lately anyways. She didn't know what he was up too but knew it had his attention hold heartily.

Nae phone buzzed letting her know a text message was waiting for her. She smiled as she read the text. She hit reply to send a message back. It was Meccah tryna talk her into going out with him later on that night. As she hit the send button the front door opened and closed letting her know Kash was home.

He walked into the living and just stood there staring at her.

"Why are you looking at me like that?" She finally asked.

"Because I can," replied Kash as he finally took a seat. "Nae, we need to talk about this."

"Kash, there's really nothing to talk about," Nae said.

"I don't wanna lose you," Kash said.

"You should have thought about that before you fucked that bitch," Nae spat.

Kash got up walking over to Nae. Pulling her up from her seat he sat down with her on his lap. This was the closest they had been to each other in a long time. It felt good having her close to him.

"Nae, at that time I didn't think I had a choice. I thought I was protecting you," Kash said turning Nae to face so that they could be looking at each other.

"Kash, you wasn't protecting me you were hurting me."

"Just give me another chance. I swear I'll make it up to you," Kash said.

"How many chances do you expect me to give you?"

Nae's phone buzzed. Kash grabbed it. "What the fuck is Meccah?" He asked looking from the phone to Nae. Nae tried snatching her phone from his hand.

"Who is Meccah?" Kash asked again as he read the text message.

"It doesn't matter who he is," Nae said getting off his lap. "Now give me my phone back."

"Are you fuckin' this nigga?" Kash asked getting up as well.

"Who I'm fuckin' doesn't concern you anymore. Just know that I'm no longer fuckin' you," she spat.

"Nae, don't fuckin' play with me!" Kash yelled grabbing her up.

"Kash, this is your entire fault. You pushed me right into the next nigga arms, remember? You cheated on me," she said reaching for her phone.

"So these are the games we're playing now?"

"Nigga, this isn't a fuckin' game. This is my life. All I ever wanted was to be happy with you but every chance you get, you fuck up my heart," Nae said.

"Say no more," Kash said as he tossed her phone clean across the room. He watched as it crashed into the wall before falling to the floor breaking.

"Why would you do that?" Nae asked getting in his face.

"I hope that nigga can do the things I couldn't for you. Just keep that nigga away from my fuckin' kids," Kash said walking off.

"Fuck you, Kash!" Nae called after him.

*

Once again Kash was pissed. Here he was trying to make things right and Nae was making plans with the next nigga. That ate him up inside. It pissed him off knowing she was willing to throw away what they were trying to build so easily. Yes he had fucked up in a major way but he still loved Nae. But how could he keep putting himself out there only to get nothing in return?

Chapter Eleven

Maria sat parked a few houses down from where Kash and Nae rest their heads. She had been watching their every move for the last two weeks. They did just about the same thing every day never doing much with each other. Kash would leave first most of the time and Nae would leave thirty minutes to an hour later. Maria never saw them with their twins, causing her to starch her head. As much as Kash praise his kids she hadn't seen him with them in two weeks causing her to wonder where they were. Maria was so deep in her thoughts she never saw or heard when her car was being approached until it was too late.

Nae smashed the crow bar into the driver's said window shattering it on impact.

"Aahh!" Maria screamed as she blocked her face from the broken glass flying everywhere.

"Why are you sitting outside my home?" Nae asked ready to swing the crow bar again this time upside Maria's head. Maria looked up at Nae smiling.

"So we meet again," she said. Nae yanked the door opened dragging her out.

"And I'm goin' to make sure this is our last time," Nae spat raising the crow bar over her head bringing it down smashing it into Maria's midsection.

"Aaaahhhhhh!" Maria grunted as she doubled over in pain.

"You got my home raided while my babies were there,"

Nae said raising the crow bar once again. Nae didn't realize she was crying until a tear rolled down her cheek.

"That....was just....the....beginning," Maria barely got out as she continued to roll around in pain. "You better.....kill me....now." she whispered.

Nae wiped the tears away. "That's just it, Maria, I don't want you dead. I want you to wish you were," Nae said beating her with the crow bar. When Maria stopped moving Nae stopped swinging. She stood over Maria huffing and puffing as her chest heaved up and down as if she had just ran a mile. Nae had just taken all her frustration and anger out on Maria. Most of it was towards her but some was for Kash. How could Nae place all the blame of Maria? Kash was the one she was in a committed relationship with not Maria.

"I hope this will teach you that fuckin' with Nae isn't where it's at," Nae said finally walking off.

Nae went into the house to change and get ready for her little outing with Meccah.

*

Kash walked into Bar 355 looking around. His eyes landed on who he was there to meet. Shyne sat at the bar watching a basketball game playing on the flat screen sitting over the bar.

"Double shot of Hennessy," Kash said approaching the bar.

"Things are that bad?" Shyne asked looking at his friend. Kash sighed as he took a seat. The bartender sat his double shot in front of him. "Keep 'em coming," he said taking the shot.

Shyne laughed.

"I lost my wife, I'm on a one way road of self-destruction and a nigga ain't have any pussy in I don't know how long," Kash said. "You tell me."

Shyne whistled. "Bruh, you down bad," Shyne laughed.

"I'm trying to fight for our relationship but we don't even talk to each other. We sleep in the same house every night but walk pass each other like we're strangers," Kash said.

Shyne had never seen Kash stressed about anything since they had known each other. He could see the stress and hurt he was carrying around. Kash really didn't want to talk about his problems anymore. He wanted nothing more for it all to be over with.

"Bruh, pack ya lady up, take her on a vacation. Just you her and the kids," Shyne said.

Kash knew a vacation wasn't going to patch things up with Nae but at this point in time any get away was fine with him.

"What up with you?" Kash asked changing the subject.

"Living, I think I finally found that special one," he laughed. "Fuck that, I know I found her."

"Word? What she's like?"

"Kendra is like no other. She got me spending any free time I do have chasing her. I mean hearing her name and seeing her smile does something to a nigga," laughed

Shyne.

"Kendra? How does she look?" Kash asked.

"Why, you know my lady or something?" Shyne asked as he searched his phone for a picture of Kendra.

"Nigga, not like that," Kash said as Shyne handed him his phone. "Her and Nae are tight as fuck," Kash told him.

"Why have I never put two and two together?" Shyne asked. "Kendra is always talkin' about her sister, Nae."

"I'm gonna warn you now. They are nothing to play with," Kash laughed for the first time in weeks. Shyne laughed too.

"Trust me I know. She warned me her damn self."

"Shyne, what up, homey?" Meccah said getting both Kash and Shyne's attention. They both turned to see who was calling Shyne.

"Oh, what up my g?" Shyne asked as they dapped each other up.

"Ain't shit just out here getting it how I live," Meccah answered looking over at Kash.

Kash laughed as he looked Meccah up and down.

"Meccah, this is my homey Kash, Kash, Meccah," Shyne introduced them.

Neither man spoke to each other as they looked each other up and down.

Shyne stood in between the two before things got out of

hand.

"Y'all two know each other or something?" He asked looked at both of them.

"Nah, that nigga grilling me like there's a problem," Meccah said.

Kash laughed, "Homey, you don't want these problems."

"It is what it is," Meccah said throwing his hands in the air.

"Meccah, holla at me later," Shyne said dapping him up again.

"A'ight, I'm meeting someone here anyway," Meccah said checking his watch. He took one last look at Kash before walking off.

"Fuck was that about?" Shyne asked when Meccah was gone.

"I don't know. I just wasn't feeling that nigga," Kash shrugged his shoulders.

"Nigga you just met him less than two minutes ago," laughed Shyne. Once again Kash shrugged his shoulders.

"It be like that sometimes," replied Kash. "Who he be anyways?"

"Man, Meccah tryna get money just like everyone else. The nigga got hella heart but the game isn't for him," Shyne answered. "He's a 26 year old wanna be." Shyne laughed. Kash did too as he looked over his should to find Meccah ordering a drink.

*

Nae strolled into bar 355 without a care in the world. She had taken most of her anger and frustrations out on Maria making her feel a whole lot better. Now she could focus on her and Meccah's so called date. It didn't matter how many times she said an outing between to friends he insisted on calling it a date. *"Some date."* She thought looking around Bar 355. If this was a way to win over her heart, Meccah was already failing by a lot.

Nae quickly spotted Meccah sitting in a booth in the corner looking good. She smiled as she switched her ass over to him. She could tell that something or someone had pissed him off.

"Why are you sitting over here with an attitude?" She asked taking her seat across from him. Meccah stared at her for a while without speaking.

"Why are you late?" He asked.

"Cause I had something to take care of. I texted you and told you that," Nae spat with an attitude of her own. "Hold up, let's get a few things straight right here and now," she said. "Whoever caused you to have that attitude; you need to take up with them. Because you are not gonna sit here talkin' to me any kind of way." She finished rolling her eyes.

"My bad ma," Meccah laughed. Nae flipped him off; she didn't find a damn thing funny. Nae ordered her first drink of the day and their little date was under way.

An hour into their date they were being interrupted. Kash roughly grabbed Nae by her arm pulling her from her seat.

"What the fuck!" Nae yelled as she pulled away from Kash

strong grip.

"Kash, stop," she said yanking away.

"So we meet again, homey," Meccah said standing to his feet. Kash ignored him as if he wasn't standing there.

"What the fuck is this?" Kash gritted looking at Nae.

"Kash, don't start," Nae said waving him off. Her day had already started off bad. She knew it was on its way to getting worst.

"Fuck you mean don't start?" He asked yanking her from her seat.

Shyne saw Meccah about to make a move.

"Homey, mind ya business," Shyne said stepping up.

"What you mean? This is my business," Meccah said looking Shyne up and down.

"It's not, you've been warned," Shyne said taking a step back.

"Kash, get ya hands off me," Nae said yanking away. Kash grabbed her forcefully pulling her towards the bathroom. All eyes were on them but he didn't give a fuck.

"KASH!" Nae wined as they walked thru the bar. Kash checked the men's room to find it empty. He pulled Nae inside with him before closing and locking the door behind him.

"So these are the games you're playing now?" He asked showing her just how pissed he was.

"What games? Kash, you fucked up not me. I told you it was over. I'm moving on and you need to do the same thing," Nae said with her hands on her hips.

"I said you can have your space. Dating other niggas was never an option," Kash said. Nae cocked her head to the side.

"Kash, who the fuck is you to tell me I can't date? Kamil, you gave me up by fuckin' that hoe but I can't see and date who I want?" Nae asked shaking her head.

"Damn, you still on that? I admitted I fucked up but we made a bond that it was gonna be us forever and a day," Kash said.

"Well you blew that," Nae said walking off. Kash grabbed her turning her to face him.

Kash and Nae just stared at each other, neither breathing a word. Kash let her go and watched as she left the bathroom. Kash knew forcing Nae to be with him wasn't the way to go. How could he be mad? When he was the reason for the bullshit they were goin' thru yet again.

"Nae," Kash called out as she walked out the bathroom. Nae turned to see what he wanted. "I love you." He said. Nae looked at him and knew he did but his actions were saying otherwise.

"I love you too," she said before leaving him standing in the bathroom alone.

*

Nae didn't know what was said between Meccah and Shyne but whatever it was she knew it wasn't pleasant.

The deep frowns they wore on their faces let her know if they wasn't standing in the middle of a bar things would have went down differently.

"I'm not feeling this anymore. I'm ready to go," Nae said as she grabbed her purse.

"Neither am I," Meccah said as he continued to grill Shyne. Shyne smiled.

"Homey you already know how I give shit up. You don't want it with me," he assured.

"And you know how I give it up. Straight G'd the fuck up," Meccah said lifting his shirt revealing the gun tucked in his waist band.

"Meccah, you a street nigga and you should know to never pull a gun if you aren't gonna use it," Shyne said basing in his face. "You already know we will be seeing each other again." He finished.

"Indeed we will. I just hope you're ready," Meccah said as he grabbed Nae's hand to leave.

"Nigga, I stay ready," Shyne assured saluting him.

Kash walked up as he watched Nae leave with Meccah.

"Son, you just gonna let ya wife walk out with the next nigga?" Shyne asked looking at Kash. "I wish Kendra would try something like that." He said walking off.

At this point in time there wasn't anything Kash could do about it. His ways was the reason Nae was in the arms of the next man.

*

Meccah walked Nae to her car. The first five minutes of the walk was a quiet one with both lost in their thoughts.

"Look, I'm sorry about what happened back there. I wasn't expecting to see him there or for him to act like that," Nae said finally saying something.

"Are you still seeing him?" Meccah asked.

"No."

"There has to be something goin' on with the two of you for him to be acting like that," Meccah said. Nae rolled her eyes.

"Meccah, we have two kids together. There's always gonna be something between us," Nae said.

"Are y'all still fuckin'?" Meccah asked as he stopped walking.

"No," Nae answered shaking her head.

"Well do you still have feeling for him?" Meccah asked looking into her face.

Nae wasn't expecting that question. She looked away as she bit into her bottom lip as she thought about the question.

"You do," Meccah said annoyed. He hadn't known Nae for that long but he was really digging the hell out of her.

"Meccah, I'm not goin' to stand here and say I don't love Kash because I do. Am I still in love with him? No, we have twin babies together so there for Kash and I will always have something in common," Nae answered.

"What I'm just a rebound for you?"

"What?" Nae laughed. "I told you I wasn't checking for any relationship. You are one cool ass dude but I just got out of a relationship and I'm not rushing into another one with you or any other nigga." Nae told him. "Don't get me wrong, I love chilling with you and talkin' to you but that's as far as it goes." She finished.

"You know what Nae, fuck you!" Meccah spat before walking off.

"Fuck you too!" Nae called after him. "You just pulled a bitch ass nigga move," she said still standing in the same spot. Meccah turned and flipped her off.

"I know you want too, ole bitch ass nigga!" Nae yelled before walking to her car.

She just knew her day couldn't get any worst. *"From here on out its fuck niggas get money."* She thought as she slipped into the driver's seat of her car.

*

To say Meccah was pissed would be an understatement. It only had been a month since him and Nae had been kicking it but he did the one thing he said he would never do and that was fall for a bitch. He felt all bitches were hoes and tricks. They used you for what they could and leave you for the next nigga with deeper pockets and better cribs. Meccah felt Nae was different from the conversations they had he knew she didn't need a nigga for anything. She made sure to let him know that. She kept herself up to par at all times. He had to have her, it didn't matter what he had to do. She had informed him of her current situation but never went into details. He could tell she still had feeling for her ex and that pissed him off. His mind was telling him to let it go but he felt he had invested a lot of time and energy dealing with her. If she didn't wanna be with him she wouldn't be with anyone.

Meccah was about to pull off but thought about it. He would sit in his ride and wait for Kash to come out of the bar. He frowned when Shyne came to mind. Shyne was a nigga he had looked up too for years, but he felt Shyne played him to the left in front of Kash and Meccah couldn't let that go either. Shyne was well known and respected around Oakland. He had the streets on smash and a team of killers that would kill at the drop of a dime. Going toe to toe with Shyne was something Meccah knew he had no wins with but he was a street nigga feeling very much disrespected and for that something had to be done.

*

Kash and Shyne stepped out of the bar letting the slight breeze brush up against their faces.

"Keep ya head up, I'm gonna holla at you later," Shyne said dapping Kash up.

"One bruh," Kash said as he watched Shyne walk off.

Drowning his problems in liquor wasn't going to solve any of the problems currently going on in his life. Kash knew that but it was an escape from reality for the moment.

Kash walked off to his car. Kash could feel someone following him. He didn't know who it was or why for that matter. Whoever it was was about to learn a lesson about following him. He patted his waist line to make sure his gun was where it was supposed to be.

Kash removed his gun turning around. "Why the fuck are you following me?" He asked causing Meccah to stop throwing his hands in the air. He wasn't expecting Kash to pull a gun on him.

"I need to holla at you about a few things," Meccah answered lowering his hands.

"Homey, there isn't a damn thing you gotta holla at me about," Kash said.

"What's up with you and Nae?" Meccah asked. Kash laughed.

"Fuck you think goin' on with us? That's wifey always will be," answered Kash. "But who the fuck is you to be questioning me about what belongs to me?"

Meccah laughed, "From the looks of things she doesn't belong to you."

"Well looks can be deceiving believe that. You may have her attention now but a nigga will always own her heart," Kash said.

"That's before I stepped into the picture," Meccah smirked.

"You don't believe that ya self," Kash said. "I was the only nigga wild enough to tame her."

"You may have been but from what I can tell you wasn't wild enough to keep her tamed," Meccah shot back.

"We shall see," Kash said pulling the trigger on the gun. He watched as the bullet flew pass Meccah's dome. "That was only a warning shot. Nigga the next time I'm sending that shit straight into ya fuckin' forehead." He assured before turning to walk away.

"Stay away from my girl," Meccah called after Kash. Kash stopped walking turning to face him once again.

"Ya girl?" Kash asked with a chuckle. "Nigga, you mean nothing. You're just another nigga tryna get what's mine. You're just another mothafucka wanting to be me. You're just another nigga who wants to see me fall, but guess what? I'm still here standing strong and I always will," Kash said.

"You're gonna fall and I'm goin' to make sure of that," Meccah said.

"I've heard it all before, look, I'm still here," Kash said waving his arms around.

"I'm gonna send you to hell where you belong."

Kash laughed once again. "Mothafucka, how can you send me somewhere I live every day? The day I take my last breath is the day I leave this life we live in called hell. No more struggle, no more drama, and no more hating ass niggas would I have to worry about anymore," Kash said. "So if you're really about that life please stop talkin' and start showing me with action because action speaks louder than words any day." He said in final walking off.

"That cocky mothafucka has got to go." Meccah thought as he watched Kash walking down the street. *"He shot at me."* He thought even more pissed.

What Meccah didn't know was that Kash had been thru the motions before. He's been down that dark road on many occasions. And like before niggas all around him had tried breaking him down only for him to come out on top. Meccah didn't know that Kash had been fighting this type of battle all his life only to become stronger and smarter.

Meccah said a silent prayer thanking god that he was still breathing. His mind was telling him to leave well enough alone but his pride and ego was telling him differently. The heat from the bullet was so close to his face when it flew pass his head. He damn near lost his cool but he had to hold up and show no fear. Coming that close to death was enough to make any nigga go to church and pray. Meccah wasn't going to anyone's church. He was out to prove a point. To who? He didn't know but it was something he felt he had to do.

*

Kash let himself into the house deep in his thoughts. He was sick and tired of it all. His entire life he was fighting the same battles just different faces. He had won many of those battles by the grace of god. This one he wasn't so sure about. If losing his life to protect the one's he loved the most was a no brainer. He would do it. Enough was enough, all he wanted to do was live happily ever after but in the crazy world he lived in there was no such things as happy ever after's.

Kash walked into the family room to find Nae laid across the couch with her kindle in her hands. He turned the light on before walking around the couch to take a seat across from her. They looked at each other before Nae continued reading her book.

"Now you are tellin' niggas about our issues?" He asked finally speaking. Nae ignored him. "Since when was that something we did?" He asked.

"Kamil, I don't know what the fuck you're talkin' about. I didn't tell anyone anything," Nae said sitting her kindle down. Kash knew she was pissed because Nae never called him by his real name.

"So what's good with you and that nigga?"

"Why does it matter?"

"Because that nigga had the nerve to approach me about you," answered Kash.

"Kamil, this is your entire fault. If you hadn't been fuckin' the next bitch for over a year behind my back we wouldn't be having these problems," Nae said sitting up.

Kash went to say something but she cut him off. "Yeah I know you said you did it for me, for us," she said rolling her eyes. "Kash, you've been fuckin' this bitch and expect me to be cool about everything. You want loyalty pussy but you got community dick," Nae said. Kash ran his hand over his face.

"And on top of that you were paying for this bitch shit. Where they do that at? You say you love me but you don't back it up with actions. You say you would never hurt me but you did. You say you hate to see me cry but you're the reason for my tears. What am I supposed to believe?" Nae asked. "You say you didn't have a choice but you did."

"Nae, how many times do you want me to say sorry? I truly am. You know I love you. You know I never wanted to hurt you. You know I hate to see you cry. But I can't change what I've done. If I could I would," Kash said.

"Kash we can sit here goin' back and forth but that will not change the fact that you fucked the next bitch," Nae said.

"My question to you is, can we move pass this?" Kash asked.

"I don't know. I love you but you hurt me deeply with this," Nae said shaking her head as she tried holding back the tears.

Kash was supposed to be the love of her life. How could he be when he did all the things he said he wouldn't?

"I respect the fact that you need time but I won't be giving up on us. I love you and that will never change. What I won't be accepting is the fact that you're talkin' to the next nigga. I don't have a valid excuse for what I did but we can't keep living in the past," Kash said. "If we're gonna move on, that's just what we're gonna do, move on."

"Why can't you let me be?" Nae asked.

"Nae," Kash said standing up. He walked over to Nae pulling her off the couch. "I put this on my kids. If you can stand here right now while lookin' me in my face and tell me that you don't wanna be with me anymore, I will never bother you again."

Nae thought on his question. She grabbed his face to look in his eyes. "Kash, I love you," she said kissing his lips. Lips she had become accustom too over the years. "But I don't wanna be with you anymore." She said releasing him. The look of sadness showed in his face and eyes, something she wasn't used to seeing.

Kash nodded his head, leaning in he kissed her lips one last time. They stood there staring into each other eyes as Kash reached into his pocket for the purple engagement ring he had brought her years ago. He grabbed her hand sitting the ring in the palm of her hand. "Do as you please with it. I have no use for it," Kash said closing her fist tightly. Their foreheads met and Kash kissed Nae's lips one last time. "Don't make the same mistakes twice," he said before walking off.

Nae finally looked down at her hand holding her engagement ring. She knew things were real. She had just told the love of her life that it was over between the two.

Chapter Twelve

Cherry stormed back into the house pissed off. She had an important meeting involving her modeling agency and was going to be late for it because Anna had sliced the tires on her car, broken all the windows out and fucked up the paint job. Cherry didn't know how she got inside the car but her white leather seats were sliced up as well.

"UGH!" Cherry screamed as she ran her hands through her hair. Something has to give. Because of this psycho bitch her kids wasn't home where they belonged causing Cherry to be on the edge at all times. She never knew what to expect or when to expect it. The ass whopping Cherry had been giving her was now a non-factor. The more she whooped her ass the more she came back. IT was as if that's what Anna wanted.

"JACQUES!" Cherry called out highly frustrated.

"What's wrong with you? I thought you were off to some meeting?" He asked walking into the kitchen shirtless.

"I was until I get outside to find all the tires slashed, my car keyed, and my windows broken out again," Cherry said looking at him pissed.

"Why you lookin' at me like that? I didn't do it," Jacques said grabbing him something to drink.

"Jacques, I know you didn't do it. That psycho ex of yours did. I'm getting real sick of this," Cherry warned.

"You don't think I am?" Jacques asked.

"Do something about it. Ques, because of this bitch my kids haven't been home in almost a month. Because of her I'm on the verge of losing my damn mind," Cherry spat very much annoyed about the entire situation.

"What am I supposed to do?" He asked taking a seat.

"How about you figure it the fuck out," Cherry said before walking off.

"Fuck wrong with him? What kind of question is that?" She thought heading to her room. She reached into her purse for her cell phone. She needed to call and cancel her meeting. She needed to get away. More than anything, she needed to see her babies.

*

Anna laughed when she saw Cherry storm back into the house pissed off. Anna knew she couldn't beat Cherry fighting wise. Hell she had gotten her ass kicked twice but that wasn't enough to stop her from causing them problems. She thought for sure that by now Cherry would have said fuck the bullshit and packed her shit to leave.

"Now that's what you call true love," mumbled Anna.

Anna knew it was time to step her game up. She was tired of the back and forth. The ass whooping was only a small price to pay for what she wanted, and that was Jacques.

The love she saw in his eyes when he spoke of Cherry or looked at her was the love she wanted him to have for her. The only problem with that was that Cherry was in her way. She knew messing up her cars and breaking into their home wasn't enough to break the two apart. Anna pulled off as she thought on what her next plan of action would be. She knew they were expecting her but they wouldn't be seeing her for a while. Because the next time they saw her, her plans would be set in motion, killing Cherry once and for all.

"I can't wait to watch that bitch blood drain from her body." Anna thought with a smile sitting on her face.

"Jacques, daddy, we will be together soon enough. You, me, and our kids." She thought.

*

Jacques walked in the room to find, Cherry lying across the bed watching TV. "You mad at me?" He asked taking a seat.

"Yes," answered Cherry. "Ques, if you would have told me about her a long time ago we wouldn't be dealing with any of this." She said sitting up.

"I know and I'm sorry about that. I wasn't expecting things to get this out of hand."

"Well they have and I'm sick of it all. Jacques, I need for you to handle that because I want my kid's home where they belong," Cherry said.

"How about we go get the kids and go on a little vacation?" Jacques asked. Cherry rolled her eyes.

"Ques, goin' on a vacation isn't goin' to solve the problem because they are still gonna be here when we get back," Cherry said.

"I know but we haven't done anything in a while and I just

wanna get away, just us," Jacques said.

"We could use a vacation," Cherry said. "When are we leaving?" She asked.

"Now," answered Jacques helping her from the bed. "We have about forty five minutes to get to the airport.

"Where are we goin'?"

"To pick up JJ and Jewel than to Jamaica," he answered.

"We're goin' to Jamaica?" Cherry asked with excitement in her voice. "Aww shit, you should have said that twenty minutes ago." Jacques laughed as he led the way out the front door.

*

On the way to the airport Cherry decided to call Nae. They hadn't talking since she had returned.

"Cherry!" Nae said answering the phone.

"What's been up with you?" Cherry asked.

"The same as always, dealing with bullshit," replied Nae.

"You and Kash still haven't handled those issues?"

"There isn't anything to handle. I told him I didn't want to be with him anymore," answered Nae.

"Nae, you didn't mean that, did you?"

"I did. Cherry, he cheated on me and told me he did it for me, for us." Cherry sighed.

"You know I don't agree with what he did but y'all love run

deeper than that. I think y'all can get pass this just like y'all got pass everything else," Cherry said hoping to talk some sense into Nae.

"I moved on. I'm talkin' to someone else," Nae said to let Cherry know how serious she was about not wanting to be with Kash anymore.

"Nae, I can hear it in your voice that you still love Kash," Cherry said.

"Cherry, you know I will always love him but I'm no longer in love with him. We tried and it didn't work out for us."

"I can't believe you're willing to throw what you two have built away just like that," Cherry said pissed.

"Who side are you on?" Nae asked.

"Yours, I just rather see you with Kash. Y'all have kids together. What about them?" Cherry asked.

"It isn't my fault. He should have thought about all of that before he did what he did," Nae said. "What's goin' on with you?" She asked changing the subject.

Cherry sighed deeply. She knew Nae was hurting but she felt what Nae and Kash had was true love and what they were going thru was just another small road block. All relationships had their ups and downs as long as you worked thru them.

"Nothing, still goin' thru the motions with this bitch, Anna," Cherry said cutting her eyes at Jacques.

Nae sighed this time. She didn't understand why they were going thru what they were going thru. If it wasn't one thing it was another.

"Bitch, you know it's gonna take way more than a crazy ex to take what's mine. I worked to fuckin' hard and been thru too much to let go, just like that," Cherry said. "And so have you and Kash."

"Cherry, you want something?" Jacques asked as they pulled into a gas station. She shook her head no as he climbed out.

"Cherry, this shit just hurts, bad," Nae said.

"I'm not saying that it doesn't. My question to you is can you see yourself not being with Kash anymore? Can you one day walk pass him and see him with another bitch draped under his arm?" Cherry asked.

"No," answered Nae.

"My point so fight for your relationship. That hoe wants what you have. Don't just hand him to her," Cherry said. "Work it out, call him and talk to him."

Nae knew Cherry was speaking the truth but it just hurt knowing Kash slept with someone else. "Cherry, I'm gonna holla at you later," Nae said.

"Okay, Ques and I are on our way to pick up my babies and we're goin' to Jamaica," Cherry informed her.

"What? I wanna go?" Nae said. Cherry laughed because she was certain Nae was on the other end of the phone pouting.

"Maybe if you and Kash get y'all shit together y'all can meet us out there with Keikeo and Lanaya," Cherry said.

Nae rolled her eyes.

She knew it was going to take more than a talk to get things right between her and Kash. She also knew that was a start.

"We'll see. Have fun and give my babies a kiss for me," Nae said before disconnecting the call.

Cherry sighed as she removed the phone from her ear looking at it. *"This is definitely what you call gangsta luv."* She thought. She just prayed they all made it to the finish line just as they did before.

Cherry closed her eyes as she laid her head back. She knew that good things never last long but she was gonna make sure her happiness lasted as long as she was breathing.

*

Jacques walked around the store as he talked on his phone.

"Fuck you want?" Ray asked when she got on the line. Brandi laughed.

"Hello to you too, mothafucka," Jacques said into the phone.

"What up?" Brandi asked still laughing.

"I need y'all help with a few things," answered Jacques.

"What isn't new? That's the only time you niggas hit us up," Ray said.

"True," Brandi said shaking her head.

"Listen, Cherry and I are on our way to Jamaica and I would like for y'all to help with this engagement I'm planning," Jacques said.

"So after all these years you're finally poppin' the question?" Brandi asked.

"It's about time," Ray said.

"Cherry was wifey from day one. The ring is just an added bonus, feel me?" He asked smiling. "She deserves that and so much more. There isn't too many females that will take on the responsibility of raising another chick baby. She did that when she could have walked away," he said. Brandi and Ray agreed.

"So what is it that you want us to do?" Ray asked.

"I just need for y'all to pick up the ring and help me plan a little engagement party," answered Jacques.

"Do we have a spending limit?" Ray asked.

"Nah, spend whatever, it's nothing."

"When do you want all this done?"

"In about a week I wanna spend some much needed time with her and my kids before y'all asses show up. Y'all know shit gonna change with y'all touch down," he laughed shaking his head.

That was one thing Jacques had always respected and loved about Cherry and her girls. Since he had met them they were all tight just as him and his boys were. Nothing would ever come between any of them. In most friendships there were one or two people jealous of the others but in this case no one was jealous of no one. How could they be jealous of each other when they all had what they wanted? Money, nice cars, big homes, and niggas with it all as well.

"I gotta go so hit me up when y'all need my card information," he said ready to hang up.

Brandi laughed. "Nigga, you should know that I can get any information I want, including your bank records. Have fun!" She laughed before hanging up. Once again Jacques shook his head. He didn't forget that Brandi could hack into anyone's bank account or records for that matter. Jacques grabbed him a bag of chips and a soda before walking to the counter.

Jacques paid for his things before leaving the store.

*

Cherry played on her phone while she waited for Jacques to return from the store.

Someone knocking on her window grabbed her attention, causing her to look up. She rolled down her window to see what the young boy wanted.

"You need help pumping the gas?" He asked.

"Thanks but no thank you," Cherry answered smiling as she started rolling the window back up. He stopped her as he looked around causing her to do the same.

"Well is there anything I can do to for you? I'm tryna make a little money," he said trying to hold her attention but it was already too late. Cherry knew he was planning on robbing her. Cherry hit the lock button before she reached under her seat for her gun. As soon as she wrapped her hand around the gun his boys approached on the other side of the car trying to open the doors.

"Are you sure this is what you wanna do?" Cherry asked the boy standing next to her. "Because I have no problem blowing ya fuckin' head off ya shoulders." She warned.

"She got a gun!" He called out to his homeys.

"And I'm not afraid to use it either. Now back the fuck up and go about your business," Cherry said. "You picked the wrong on to try and rob today."

"I don't want any problems," he said with his hands in the air as he slowly backed up.

Cherry kept the gun trained on him.

Jacques walked out the store and the first thing he saw were the gun and a group of young niggas backing away from his ride. He dropped his bag jogging their way.

"What the fuck goin' on?" He asked grabbing the boy Cherry was holding the gun on by the back of his neck. "Babe, are you good?" He asked looking at Cherry.

"I'm fine, let's go," she said lowering her gun.

"Y'all lil' niggas tried robbing my lady?" He asked looking at all four of them.

"No," the boy he was holding answered quickly.

Cherry could see the fire in Jacques eyes. "Baby, let it go and come on we have a flight to catch," she said.

Jacques didn't take kindly to anyone fucking with his lady

or his kids for that matter. They young boy had crossed the line and disrespected his woman and he had to be taught a lesson. Jacques punched him in his stomach and he folded in half before falling to the ground.

"Ayo, fall back," one of the boy partners said stepping up. Cherry opened her door with her gun in her hand.

"No, mothafucka you fall back," she said holding the gun for him to see.

"Aaaahhhhhhh!" The boy screamed out as Jacques smashed his fingers with his sneaker. He was trying to break his entire hand.

"JACQUES!" Cherry called out. "Let's fuckin' go," she spat.

"Next time you niggas won't be so fuckin' luck," Jacques warned walking off. Cherry slipped back into the passenger seat while Jacques jumped into the driver's seat. They pulled off without speaking another word.

"I should have bodied that nigga," Jacques said.

"No you shouldn't have. Jacques we are already dealing with bullshit. We don't need you facing another murder charge, remember that?" Cherry asked.

"They tried to rob you. There isn't no tellin' what would have happened if I didn't come out the store," he said pissed.

"Babe, I can take care of myself. Trust me, the only thing that would have happened was one or all of 'em would have been bleeding from a bullet hole," Cherry laughed.

"I know you can take care of yourself. But that's what you

have me for," Jacques said getting more pissed off thinking about it.

"Can we just let it go so that we can go get out babies and enjoy ourselves in Jamaica?" Cherry asked playing with his dreads.

Jacques didn't say anything else about what had went down at the gas station as they drove to the airport.

Chapter Thirteen

Kash sat at the island nursing his spiked coffee. He had been in New York for the past few days. He felt there was no need for him to be in California. He and Nae were officially over. Kash smiled thinking about when he had first met Nae. It was the summer time, he would have never thought they would have made it this far. But it was fate that brought them together. He always knew she was the one but her holding back from fear of being hurt. It took him some time but he had finally broken the thick ice she had formed around her heart, only the let her down once again. Being shot five times didn't compare to the pain that ripped thru his heart from the thought of him losing the love of his life.

Sex ain't better than love by Trey Songz came to mind and Kash had to agree whole hearty. Sex was never better than love, especially if you had found the right one to love you.

"What are you doin' here?" Lisa asked walking into the kitchen to find Kash sitting with his head hung low as if he had just lost his dog.

"I came to get my babies," he answered never looking up.

"You look like shit, boy," she said grabbing a few pots and pans from the cabins.

"Ma, she's gone," Kash said.

"And whose fault is that?" Lisa asked looking at him.

"Mine," was his reply.

"She gave me my walkin' papers and told me she didn't wanna be with me anymore," Kash said. Lisa sighed.

"Have she packed ya shit? Have she told you to leave?" Kash shook his head no. "It isn't over than," Lisa said.

"But she's seeing another nigga," Kash informed her.

"Kash, that nigga don't mean shit. She's hurting and wants you to see it. She wants you to hurt just as much as you hurt her. Nae loves you, she wants you to see how it feels to be hurt," Lisa said. "You and Jacques kill me. As soon as something goes wrong, y'all mothafuckas act like it's the end of the world. Man up and do what you gotta go, fight for what you want. Nothing in life if easy especially a relationship," she said shaking her head.

"I know-"

"Act like you know and stop walking around like your life is over. If y'all niggas stop thinking with ya dick and start using ya head you wouldn't have half the problems you have," Lisa said as she moved around the kitchen.

"What caused all of this anyways?" She asked.

Kash ran everything down.

"I would have given you your walking papers too. Kash, you've been fuckin' another bitch for over a year and paid for her surgery and brought her a home?" Lisa asked in disbelief. "But you don't see anything wrong with that?"

"I didn't say that," Kash sighed. "At the time I thought I was doin' what I had to do to protect, Nae."

"Kash, you really believe that fuckin' the next bitch was

protecting, Nae?" Lisa asked looking at him. "You know what don't answer that." She said waving him off.

"Grandma, we hungry," Keikeo said running into the kitchen. "Daddy!" He screamed when he saw Kash. Kash smiled for the first time in a long time as he got up to pick his son up. "Where's mommy?" He asked forgetting all about being hungry.

"I came to get you and Lanaya to take y'all to see, mommy," Kash answered as he hugged his baby boy.

Keikeo got down as he ran to get his sister. "Lanaya, we going to see mommy," he said as he ran out of the kitchen.

"Kash, it isn't just about you and Nae anymore. You two have them two to worry and think about now," Lisa said as she pointed out the kitchen.

"Trust me I know. Which is why I'm goin' home to handle my business and win my woman back," he replied.

"Daddy, are we really going home?" Lanaya asked running into the kitchen. She was too happy to see her daddy.

"Yes, princess we are goin' home," Kash answered picking her up.

"Bye-bye grandma," she said waving to Lisa.

"You aren't gonna stay for breakfast?" Lisa asked.

"I'm gonna have to take a rain check," Kash said as he picked Keikeo up too. "Ma, thanks for everything. Call me if you need anything," he said as he walked over to give Lisa a kiss on the cheek.

"Boy, you know I'm fine and will always be. What I need for you to do is get your shit right at home," she said hugging him.

"Ohh, grandma said a bad word," Lanaya said giggling as she buried her face into Kash neck. Lisa and Kash both laughed.

"I don't know who's the worst out of her or Jewel. They both have mouths on them," Lisa said shaking her head yet again.

"They get that from their mommas. Speaking of which, where is Jewel and JJ?" Kash asked.

"Cherry and Jacques came to get them a couple days ago. They went on a little family vacation," answered Lisa. Kash nodded his head.

"I love you, ma," Kash said as he headed for the door with his kids in his arms.

"I love you too," Lisa called after him as she watched him leave.

She was glad the kids were all gone but she knew she was going to missed them.

*

Nae hasn't seen Kash since the day she had told him it was over. It wasn't something she was use too. She would be lying if she said she didn't miss him. She was still hanging with Meccah every chance she got. He was cool and she loved his company, but he wasn't Kash. She knew he was starting to catch feelings. Even after she told him it would be nothing more between the two. That didn't stop him from trying.

Being that she had a lot of free time on her hands, she began putting her attention back on opening her day care; she had planned to open years ago. Nae felt bad, she hadn't seen or talked to her babies in weeks. But because of the things that was going on she rather them stay where they was. She made a mental note to make sure she flew down to New York to see them at the end of the week.

"Hello?" Nae said answering her ringing phone.

"What you been up too?" Kendra asked. "We haven't talked in a while."

"I know. I've just been tryna get my day care open, finally," answered Nae. "What's been up with you?"

"Falling in love," replied Kendra with a little chuckle.

"Bitch bye, ya ass been fell," Nae laughed. Kendra laughed too.

"True, it's as if he has a spell on me or something."

"Nah, he doesn't. That's just true love," answered Nae. She knew the feeling all too well. She felt the same way when she and Kash had first met each other. He had swept her off her feet when no one else could. He knew what to say when to say it and how to say it.

"How are things with you and Kash?" Kendra asked.

Not good and I'm not gonna sit here and lie like I don't miss him, because I do," Nae said. "I just feel if I give him a pass for this one, he will think it's okay for what he did."

"He knows he fucked up, he knows that and so does everyone else. But, if y'all are gonna be together and make it work, y'all need to stop playing all these games," Kendra said.

"How can we live happily ever after when it's like no one wanna see us together? If it isn't one thing it's another," Nae said.

"Sis, fuck what everyone else thinks or feel. All that matters is that you and Kash love each other and y'all know for a fact that it can work," Kendra said. "When y'all get pass this bullshit it's gonna be another bitch down the road wanting what you have and will do anything to get it. It's gonna be up to you and Kash to prove that y'all bond is strong enough not to be broken." She finished.

"It just hurt knowing that bitch had that much power over my man," Nae sighed.

"It couldn't have been that much power because you see who he's still chasing after, you. You're the one he wants to be with for the rest of his life. You're the one with his kids, the house, the ring, and him," Kendra said. "She sees and knows that. She wants what you have, badly."

Nae heard the door open and close. She could hear two voices talking in a low whisper. "Kendra, I'm goin' to call you back. My babies are home," Nae said hanging up not giving her a chance to respond.

Nae got up rushing to meet them at the door. "Oh god, I miss you," she said as she grabbed Keikeo and Lanaya from Kash arms.

"Mommy!" They both sung as they wrapped their arms

around her neck. Kash took a step back to admire the Kodak moment. He hadn't seen Nae smile in months and it was good as hell to see it again.

"Are y'all gonna tell me all about your vacation?" Nae asked as she put them down. She grabbed their hands walking into the living room with them. She turned to mouth the words "Thank you." to Kash. Who simply nodded his head before walking off. He knew they needed to have a heart to heart conversation about them and their relationship but he would wait giving Nae time to spend the Keikeo and Lanaya, first.

*

Kash went upstairs to shower and change his clothes. He rolled him a blunt as he watched ESPN. Kash smoked his blunt as his mind wondered. It had been a while since Maria called or even showed up. He knew that wasn't a good sign and he needed to know what she was up too. He grabbed his cell to call Chase.

"What up?" Chase answered on the third ring.

"I need for you to trace a phone number for its location," Kash said.

"What's the number?" Chase asked. Kash ran it back to him. "A'ight, I'll have something for you in about an hour." Chase said hanging up.

Kash finished the blunt and made himself more comfortable in bed. This was the first night he had laid in his bed. *"I gotta get my shit together."* He thought.

A couple hours later Nae walked into the room with a

smile on her face. They locked eyes for a second before she continued moving around the room. Kash watched her without speaking a word. He never took his eyes off her until she walked into the bathroom closing the door behind her.

"Yeah, she's still pissed with a nigga." He thought running his hands over his face.

Thirty minutes later Nae reappeared wrapped in only a towel. Once again Kash couldn't take his eyes off her. "Where are the kids?" He asked.

"Sleep, thanks for bringing my babies home," Nae said.

"There's really no thanks needed. You know we need to talk, right?"

"I'm listening," Nae said as she grabbed her favorite scented lotion. Nae sat on the edge of the bed applying lotion to her body as she waited to hear what Kash had to say this go round.

"I don't know how many times you want me to say I'm sorry, because I really am. Hurting you is something I never planned on doin'," Kash said. "All I know is that I love you and can't see myself living without you. He finished.

"I love you too, you know that but I don't know if I can forgive you for this. What if another bitch decides to blackmail you, than what?" Nae asked.

"I can promise you that there will never be another bitch," Kash said. "I'm not asking for you to forget what I've done all I want you to do is forgive me so that we can move on pass this. So that we can get back to us and our kids," he said.

"Kash, I'm willing to move pass this because we have been thru worst shit than this and I can't see myself living without you," Nae said causing Kash to smile.

Kash got up from the bed walking over to where Nae was. He stood in front of her as they stared each other down. This was the closest they had been to each other in a long time. Both of them unsure of what to do next.

"Where's your engagement ring?" Kash asked looking her in the eyes.

"On my dresser," Nae answered.

"Go get it and put it back," Kash demanded. Nae got up and did as she was told.

She wiggled her fingers in his face. "Happy?" Kash nodded his head that he was.

"Come here," he said waving her over. He hadn't touched her in a while and was about to make up for lost time.

Once again Nae did as she was told, walking over to where Kash stood she stood in front of him waiting for him to make the next move.

Kash removed the towel letting it fall to the floor as they locked eyes. He picked Nae up with ease carrying her around the bed. He laid her down trailing kisses from her neck down to her other set of lips. Nae body quickly responded to his touches. He was the only nigga that could put her body in submission.

"Kash!" Nae moaned as his tongue connected to her

throbbing pearl. Kash lapped at her pearl showing her what she's been missing.

Kash ran his snake like tongue up and down her lips slowly sending shivers up and down Nae's spine, as he massage her clit with his thumb.

"Oh shit, baby waittttt!" Nae screamed as she tried closing her legs. Kash held her tights in place with a firm grip keeping them where he needed them to be, out his way.

"I don't need to wait for nothing, what I need for you to do is cum for me," Kash said speaking into her pussy before he dived back in.

Kash didn't have to wait long as he used his tongue swirling it around in circular motions before wrapping his full lips around her clit sucking on it as if it was a popsicle on a hot summer day.

"Oh my god, Kasssshhhhhhhh!" Nae moaned as her love juices rushed from within landing on Kash face making his face look like a glazed donut. Kash smiled as he watched Nae body twitch and shake uncontrollable. He knew his tongue was still up to par.

Kash removed his jeans before going back in for seconds. He wasn't gonna stop until she either begged or passed out. Whichever came first. He wanted to remind her that there was no other nigga like him. Living or dead, he was a one of a kind type of nigga and she had lucked up. Yes, Kash was that damn cocky.

Kash pulled Nae to the edge of the bed throwing one of her legs over his shoulder as he begin pleasing her with his tongue once again. Kash slid one finger inside as he continued to use the tip of his tongue to please her orally. He slid his finger in and out of her love tunnel slowly as her love juices coded his finger. Nae was wetter than a mothafucka; Kash loved every minute of it.

"Aww fuck, just like that, I'm about to cum again, Meccah!" Nae called out. Her body quickly tensed up as her heart beat loudly in her chest. *"Oh god, I know I didn't say that out loud."* Nae thought to afraid to open her eyes.

"What the fuck did you just say?" Kash asked standing up.

Nae shook her head from side to side as tears escaped her eyes. "I'm sorry," she whispered not knowing what else to say.

"You fucked that nigga?" Kash asked yanking Nae from the bed. Answer me damn it!" Kash yelled as he shook her.

"No, I never fucked him, I swear," Nae said not wanting to look Kash in his face.

"What was that? Some type of pay back for me fuckin' Maria?" Kash asked. "What you were planning on fuckin him or something?" He asked as he redressed. He was beyond pissed.

"Really, Kash, if I wanted payback I would have fucked him already and no I wasn't planning on fuckin' him. That's just it I don't want him I want you," Nae said as she walked off. She stopped and faced him again. "It doesn't matter how many times I say I'm over you I'm not or how many times I say it's over I just can't get you off my mind and my heart won't let me let you go," she said. "That's the difference between you and I. I have self-control. I did what I said I wouldn't and that was given another nigga my heart. You have it and it knows nothing but you." She finished before walking into the bathroom slamming the door behind her.

Kash wanted to go after her but his pride was standing in the way. Lord knows he loved her but she has just played the fuck outta him by calling out the next nigga's name while he was pleasing her.

"She could have fucked him but she didn't." His mind threw at him. Kash sucked his teeth as he continued to dress. He needed to take a ride to clear his mind.

Kash looked over at the bathroom door before leaving the room. He shook his head as he walked out the room.

*

Nae felt bad about what she had said, she didn't mean it nor did she know where that came from. She would be lying if she said she hadn't thought about messing around with Meccah but the love she had for Kash would never let her cross that line.

At least I didn't fuck him. She thought looking herself over in the mirror.

Nae was starting to feel as if she was fighting a losing battle. Giving up was something she never did but she was really getting sick and tired of the back and forth. One day they were happy and the next they wasn't.

"All relationships have their ups and downs." Her mind threw at her. She knew that was the truth. Nae got in the shower with a heavy heart.

*

Kash find himself pulling up to Shyne's crib. He thought about calling Jacques but he didn't want to interrupt his vacation or family time. He would just fill him in when they linked up again. *"I hope he's dealing with his issues much better than I am."* Kash thought as he shut off his ride stepping out.

Kash slowly walked to the front door and knocked twice. He took a step back while he waited for Shyne to answer.

"Who you be?" Shyne asked from the other side of the door.

"Nigga, it's me," Kash said. Shyne unlocked and opened the door.

"Fuck you want?" Shyne asked looking over his shoulder.

"Are you busy or something?" Kash asked as he stepped inside.

"Truthfully yeah, Kendra and I are in the middle of something," Shyne smiled as he closed the door. From the look on Kash face he knew something had gone wrong between him and Nae once again. That was the only time he walked around with the puppy dog face.

"You need a drink, huh?" Shyne asked as they walked to the kitchen. Kash nodded his head up and down. "What happen now?"

Kash sighed. "Nigga, she called me Meccah while I'm giving her head," Kash said straight up. Shyne whistled as he sat a cup in front of Kash. He went to the cabinet once again grabbing a bottle of Hennessy.

"Will this do?" Shyne asked holding the bottle up.

"Anything will do right about now," answered Kash.

"Shyne?" Kendra said coming into the kitchen tying her robe closed.

"What up, Kendra?" Kash asked.

"Nothing much, shouldn't you be home working things out with Nae?" She asked.

"Ma, let me holla at my nigga. I'll be upstairs in a few," Shyne said smacking her on the ass.

"Please hurry up, Ice is waiting," she winked as she walked out the kitchen.

"Who the fuck is Ice?" Kash asked looking at Shyne.

"Nigga, that's something you don't have to worry about," laughed Shyne.

"I'm up," Kash said grabbing the bottle. "Good lookin'." He said holding the bottle up.

"Are you sure?" Shyne asked.

"Yeah, nigga, handle ya business. At least one of us is," Kash spat as he walked out the front door. Getting in his ride he pulled off with no real destination in mind.

Chapter Fourteen

Cherry and Jacques had been in Jamaica for the past week enjoying each other and their kids. It had been a non-stressful week for the both of them and they were truly happy. Cherry stood on the deck watching the sun set; it was a beautiful sight to see. That didn't stop her from worrying about the bullshit they would have to face when they got back home. She knew they wouldn't be able to live happy with Anna still breathing. It would all ball down to one of them losing their lives at the end.

Jacques stepped out on the deck wrapping his arms around her waist. Cherry smiled.

"Are the kids sleeping?" She asked.

"Finally," laughed Ques. "What's the matter?" He asked turning Cherry to face him. He could feel that something was bothering her. "And please don't say nothing is bothering you. You don't want me lying to you so don't lie to me."

"I'm just worried about when we get back home," answered Cherry.

Jacques sighed running his hand over his face. "Babe, you aren't supposed to be worrying about anything," he said becoming a little pissed.

"How can you say that when you have a crazy ex coming after me every chance she gets?" Cherry asked getting an attitude of her own.

"Because she is someone I have to deal with. I didn't mean

for things to get out of hand nor was I expecting to ever see her or for any of this to play out like it's playing out," Jacques said.

"Corrections, we have to deal with her. You aren't in a relationship alone, Jacques," Cherry said pointing from herself to him.

"I know but-"

"There are no buts. We are in this together. Which means if you have a problem so do I," Cherry said cutting him off.

"You're right," Jacques said pulling her into his chest. "Can we please forget about all that and focus on us?" He said looking into her pretty brown eyes.

"I can do that," answered Cherry.

"Good, the kids are sleep and I'm tryna play a few grown up games," Jacques said pulling her back into the house. Jacques didn't give her a chance to respond as he kissed her lips while he walked backwards to the bed. Jacques laid Cherry on the bed before he dropped to his knees. He didn't waste any time removing her cherry red thongs, he simply slid them to the side and begin feasting on her kitty. Jacques used his tongue like it was a navigation system and he was trying to find his destination around Cherry's love box. Jacques didn't need a navigation system because he knew where he was and he knew what it took to please his woman.

"Ques, baby!" Cherry moaned as she ran her hands thru his dreads.

"What the hell I tell you about pulling on my dreads like

that?" He asked coming up for air.

"Sorry," Cherry laughed.

There was a knock on the door. "Daddy," they heard Jewel say with sleep in her voice.

Both Jacques and Cherry was pissed. Cherry laughed from the face Jacques made as he got up making his way to the door. "And you want another one," Cherry said. Cherry rolled over and made herself more comfortable. She knew it would be a while before Jacques returned.

"What are you doin' up?" Jacques asked as he picked her up.

"I want to lay with you and mommy," Jewel said as she laid her head on his shoulder.

"Not tonight, baby," Jacques said as he walked her back to her room. He laughed when he found JJ knocked out across his bed.

Jacques laid Jewel back in her bed covering her up. "Daddy, lay with me," she said as she tried to keep her eyes open. Jacques did as she asked and she wrapped her little arms around his neck closing her eyes.

Jacques laid back and thought about everything he had been thru over the last few years. He had almost lost his life and missed out on being a father. That thought alone always bothered him. There was no greater feeling then being a father. He loved it, knowing that his kids loved him unconditionally. When all else failed they would always be the reason he stride to be a better man, a better father, and a better person. When his days seemed dark and cold all it took was one look at his babies and everything else seem so small.

*

Brandi and Ray had been running around for the past week nonstop doing all the things Jacques had asked them to do.

"Do you think Cherry gonna like this ring?" Brandi asked as she admired the ring herself.

"If she don't I do," Ray laughed.

"Word," Brandi agreed.

"Now all we have to do is get everyone to Jamaica," Ray said.

"That is the easiest part," Brandi said as she picked up her phone. "When are we planning to leave again?" She asked.

"Tomorrow morning. Everyone tickets are already reserved," answered Ray.

"Dani, a vacation to Jamaica on Jacques, are you down?" Brandi laughed.

"Hell yeah, when do we leave?" Dani asked on the other end.

"I told you," Brandi mouth to Ray.

"You and King tickets are already reserved for tomorrow morning," Brandi answered.

"Why, what's goin' on?" Dani asked.

"He's planning on asking Cherry to marry him and he wants us all there," answered Brandi.

"Aye, that's what's up. I'll see you in Jamaica," Dani said.

"Dani, what up?" Ray asked in the background.

"Oh shit, what's good with you, Ray?" Dani asked.

"Not much, just tryna get my baby girl from this nigga, Melo," Ray laughed but was dead serious.

"Let me find out that nigga soldiers don't march," laughed Dani.

"Bitch, don't play. I swear I asked that nigga that the other day," Ray said. "If they don't that nigga gotta hit the road."

Brandi and Dani were in tears. "That's fucked up," Brandi said. "Don't play my nigga like that."

"That nigga bet not play. Matter fact when we get back we're goin' straight to the doctor's office," Ray said. Once again her girls were rolling.

"You are a cold piece of work," Dani said.

"Shit, y'all know I keep it real at all times," Ray said shrugging her shoulders.

"Y'all think them Jamaicans are ready for us?" Dani asked.

"Hell no!" Ray and Brandi said at the same time.

"Y'all know how the news report how a storm is on its way but nobody believes it because the sun is shining?" Ray asked. "Well that's up. Someone needs to warn them mothafuckin' Jamaicans because we are about to turn

Jamaica out, baby!" Ray laughed.

"Ray, call Vonne while I dial Nija. I haven't talked to either of them in a while," Brandi said as she put Dani on hold to call Nija. Ray called Vonne putting her on speaker.

"Oh bitch you remember me?" Vonne asked when she came on the line.

"Bitch, the phone works both ways," Ray replied.

"Hey," Nija said answering her phone.

"Ladies, we have been invited to Jamaica all expensive paid," Brandi said.

"When we leave?" Nija asked laughing.

"Right," Vonne laughed. "Everything already paid for. Who can say no to that?"

"Jacques has paid for everything. He's planning to ask Cherry to marry him and he wants us all there," Brandi said once again.

"Finally, one of them niggas are getting shit right," Vonne said.

"Right, so when we leave?" Nija asked.

"Oh shit, nigga wait," Dani said.

"Hell no, I told you not to answer the fuckin' phone anyways," King said in the background. "So you can either hang up now or they can get an ear full of something serious." He finished.

"Ladies, I gotta go. I'll see y'all in Jamaica," Dani laughed as she disconnected the call.

"Get it bitch!" Vonne said.

"Ladies, I will holla at y'all when we get to Jamaica. A bitch is tired as hell," Brandi said.

"A'ight, later," Nija said hanging up.

"So that's it? I only get a two minute conversation with you hoes?" Vonne asked. "Y'all make me feel like a cheap hoe at times," she laughed. "It's all good though, one."

Brandi and Ray looked at each other before busting out laughing.

"I don't know whose mouth is worst out of you, Vonne, or Nae's," Brandi said getting up from her seat.

Ray laughed. "I'll take that cause I don't give a fuck what I say outta my mouth," she said shrugging her shoulders.

*

Jacques tucked Jewel and JJ in before he left their room. Walking back into his room he found Cherry knocked out. "Ain't this about a bitch," he sighed. He had half the mind to wake her up so that they could finish what they started but he was gonna let her sleep. She would be making it up to him another time. He removed his clothes and before climbing into the bed with Cherry. He kissed her on her forehead as he whispered I love you before he closed his eyes.

The next morning Cherry got up first. She got herself together before checking on JJ and Jewel. She smiled when she found them still sleep. *"Good."* She thought. She felt bad about falling asleep on Jacques last night and plan to make it up to him right now. She walked back to her room making sure she locked the door behind her. She just prayed JJ and Jewel stayed sleep long enough for anything to go down.

Cherry removed her robe as she walked to the bed. Jacques was knocked out cold spread across the bed. He was sleep as if he hadn't slept in days. Cherry knew just what would wake him up.

Cherry pulled his boxers down enough to release his member. She wrapped both hands around it as she teased the tip of his dick with her tongue. Jacques grunted but never opened his eyes. She knew she would have to apply a little more pressure to wake him. She wrapped her mouth around his dick as she continued to jerk him off.

Jacques eyes popped open, he sat up. "Morning babe, lay back and enjoy," she smiled as she continued to work him over.

"It's gonna be a great fuckin' morning," Jacques said as he threw his hands behind his head.

Five minutes into it Jacques stopped Cherry. My turn he said pulling her up. He went to kiss her but she stopped him. "Nah, nigga you got that morning breathe," Cherry laughed but was dead serious.

"Really, you gonna make me go brush my teeth with a hard dick?" He asked. She nodded her head up and down. Jacques shook his head as he got up to brush his teeth, dick hard as a missile.

"Damn nigga!" Cherry said as Jacques pulled her to the

edge of the bed. He opened her robe to find she had nothing on underneath it. He smiled as he found her second pair of lips. He would finish what he started the night before.

"Ques, can I just get the dick before the kids decide to wake up?" Cherry asked, not wanting to be deprived of getting her shirt off yet again.

Jacques threw both her legs over his shoulders and slide deep inside of Cherry love box.

"Aaaahhh!" Cherry moaned gripping the sheets. Jacques continued to slide in and out of Cherry with a smile on his face. He loved watching his dick slide in and out of his lady. It turned them both on.

"Ques stop playing and make me cum," Cherry begged as he rammed his dick in and out at a nice pace. Jacques removed her legs from over his shoulders flipping her on her stomach. He quickly pulled her up on her knees never missing a beat as he placed her hands behind her back.

"How bad do you wanna come all over this dick?" He asked smacking her on the ass.

"Oh shit, bad baby," Cherry moaned as she pulled him in even deeper.

"Awe shit!" Jacques grunted as she squeezed her pussy muscle around his dick. "Shit," he said as sweat formed on his forehead.

"Ques stop playing and make me cum," Cherry damn near begged.

Jacques fucked Cherry slowly, as she begged for more. He

picked up his pace as she tried scooting away.

"Fuck you goin'?" He asked holding her legs tighter keeping her when he needed her to be.

Jacques flipped her on her stomach before he pulled her up on her knees. Grabbing a hold of her waist with both hands he dug in deep.

"Aaahhh fuck!" Cherry moaned as she buried her face into the sheets.

Cherry flipped her hair as she threw it back winding her hips in slow motion matching Jacque rhythm. Jacques leaned in kissing Cherry all over her back. His mouth connected to the back of her neck, he gently bit her sending chills down her entire body.

A few minutes later they both were coming with each other, collapsing on the bed beside each other.

Chapter Fifteen

Kash and Meccah tussled for the gun, both men were breathing heavily. Neither of them knew how long they had been going at it. Time wasn't the concern, getting the gun was. Both their lives were on the line. Kash twisted Meccah's arms.

"Aaaahhhhhh!" Meccah screamed as the gun fell from his hand sliding clean across the room. Him and Kash looked at each other and back at the gun. Meccah elbowed Kash in his face drawing blood. Kash head jerked back but that wasn't enough to stop him from grabbing Meccah slamming him into the floor. Kash punched Meccah in his face twice tryna force him to stay down. But he wasn't giving up that easy. Kash jumped to his feet bringing his foot up to stomp Meccah in his stomach. Meccah doubled over in pain as Kash brought his foot down smashing it into the side of his head. That blow damn near knocked Meccah out but he was still breathing, in a lot of pain and dazed. Kash went for the gun but Meccah tripped him with his foot. Meccah grabbed Kash legs climbing over him going after the gun. Kash flipped Meccah off him but it was too late, Meccah had grabbed the gun jumping to his feet. He quickly pointed the gun at Kash head.

"What up now?" Meccah asked with a bloody grin on his face.

Kash stood to his feet unfazed of the gun being pointed to his face. This wasn't the first time a gun had been pointed at him. It was all a part of the life he used to live.

"Mothafucka you tell me," Kash spat. "You're the one with the gun."

"I am," Meccah laughed. The front door opening and closing grabbed both their attention.

"Daddy!" Lanaya and Keikeo yelled as she ran thru the house.

"Why I gotta keep tellin' y'all little asses about running in the house?" Nae asked causing them to stop running.

All three entered into the living room unaware of what was going on.

Nae stopped when she found Meccah and Kash standing toe to toe. "What's goin' on?" She asked looking from Kash to Meccah.

"Daddy!" Keikeo and Lanaya screamed.

"NO!" Kash screamed stopping them from running to him. "Nae, get them outta here."

Nae was at a loss for words. She was stuck and didn't know what to do. "NAE!" Kash screamed getting her attention. She looked over at him with tears in her eyes.

"Get my babies and get the fuck outta here!" Kash barked never taking his eyes off Meccah.

Meccah smiled as he turned his gun on Nae and the kids.

"No!" Nae screamed as she grabbed her babies.

"Meccah, you want me dead so here I am," Kash said holding his hands in the air. His stomach knotted seeing what Meccah had planned. "Nae leave now!" Kash said taking a step closer to Meccah. He needed for Meccah to turn the gun on him so that his family could make it out safely.

Nae grabbed her babies so that she could take them too safely. Meccah pulled the trigger twice.

"NOOOOOOO!" Kash screamed as everything seems to be going in slow motion. Kash could see the bullet leaving the gun and the smoke left behind. Kash charged Meccah but wasn't quick enough as he turned the back on him pulling the trigger two more times. That didn't stop Kash from going after him as the bullets ripped thru his chest. The burning he felt inside wasn't enough to stop him. The pain and hurt sitting in his heart was enough to keep him going.

Kash fought with all he had. He could feel all his energy leaving his body. His eyes blurred as he started seeing double. He closed his eye trying to shake it off but it didn't help only causing him to become even dizzier.

Meccah punched Kash in his face twice as he stumbled backwards. Kash tried charging him but he didn't know which way to go. It was as if Meccah multiplied.

Kash heard when Meccah let off another shot. He wasn't sure if he had shot him again being that his body had already gone numb. Nae screaming is what got his attention.

"OH GOD, NOOOOOOOOOO!" Nae screamed.

Meccah smiled seeing the hurtful look on Nae's face.

"This is what that gangsta luv will get you," Meccah spat ready to pull the trigger once again. Kash dropped to his knees as he tried holding on to his life. Once again he was on the verge of losing his life by the hands of a jealous man. "Nae, you played with a nigga emotions and this is the end result." He said aiming the gun at Lanaya this time.

"NOOOOOO!" Nae screamed as she tried shielding Lanaya from harm's way but she wasn't quick enough as the bullet penetrated her little body.

"This is life," Meccah said shrugging his shoulders. He turned to Kash just as he fell face first into the floor. Meccah pulled the trigger on Kash until the clip was empty.

Nae gasped as she sat up in bed. She looked around her dark room as sweat dripped from her forehead. He turned on the lamp next to her bed looking around. She found that Kash wasn't lying beside her. She flipped the covers off her rushing to check on Keikeo and Lanaya. The dream she had moments ago felt too real. She knew she had to do something because things were only going to get worst for her and Kash. They needed to make up their minds soon. They either wanted to be with each other or they didn't.

Nae opened the kid's room door to find their room empty. She began to panic when she didn't see them sleeping in their beds. She closed their room door back running downstairs.

Nae heard the front door open and close. "Kash, where are my babies," she asked running to him with tears in her eyes.

"What's wrong?" He asked.

"My babies, Kash, they aren't sleeping in their room," Nae cried.

"Nae, Kendra came to get them," answered Kash. "What happened?"

Nae sighed a huge sigh of relief but the tears never stopped falling.

"I have to go get my babies," she said turning to run. Kash grabbed her before she could take off turning her around to face him once again. And again he stood there looking into Nae's eyes where he saw hurt, pain, and worry.

"What has you on the verge of a nervous break-down?" He asked using his thumbs to wipe her tears away.

Nae wrapped her arms tightly around Kash neck squeezing him as if that would be the last hug they shared. "Oh god, please tell me this is real?" She asked not wanting to let go.

"It's real. What's the matter?" He asked again. Kash knew whatever it was had to be crazy. Since him and Nae had been dating he had never seen her nervous about anything. Her body was trembling.

"Kash, we gotta figure this shit out," Nae said finally letting him go to look in his face. "I just had a dream you and my babies got killed right in front of me," she cried.

"What?" Kash asked.

"I need to go get my babies," Nae said walking off to get dress.

"Nae, they are safe," Kash assured grabbing her again.

"Kamil, that dream I had felt so surreal. I sat and watched this nigga kill you and my babies in front of me. I just wanna hold them," Nae said,

Kash pulling Nae into him wrapping his arms around her.

"Babe, I swear we're gonna get thru this," Kash said hugging Nae as he rocked her back and forth.

"How could you be so sure?" She asked.

"Because, not only have we made it thru worst shit than this but because the love we have for each other is just that strong," Kash said.

"Kash, we need to get away. I wanna go get my babies and take a trip just us," Nae said looking up into his eyes.

"No, us running every time something happen isn't gonna solve shit," Kash said.

"But Kash, he's gonna kill you, Lanaya, and Keikeo," Nae said breaking down once again.

"Who is he?" Kash asked.

"Meccah, it happened right here," she said pointing. "You two were fighting for the gun and we walked in unaware of what was goin' on," Nae said.

"Listen, you and the kids can go stay with Kendra until I find and kill this nigga. But I'm not running or goin' anywhere," Kash said. "A'ight, let me make a few calls and we can leave," He said releasing her.

Nae nodded her head walking off.

Kash sighed deeply and knew things had to give. He called

Chase first.

"Nigga, why the fuck are you callin' me this late for?" Chase answered his phone.

"Because I need you to do me a favor," Kash answered.

"And this couldn't wait until the morning?"

"No, I can't explain anything right now. I need for you to get me that last known address this nigga Meccah had," Kash said into the phone.

"Give me like ten minutes," Chase said hanging up.

Kash looked around running his hands thru his waves. Life was definitely a bitch.

"I'm ready to go," Nae said now standing in a pair of sweats, air max sneakers.

"Let's go," Kash said grabbing her hand as they headed out the door.

On the way to the Kendra crib, Nae called her to let her know she was on her way.

*

When Shyne made it home he found Kendra still up watching TV.

"What are you still doin' up?" He asked removing his shirt.

"After cooking like you asked me too, and running around with Lanaya and Keikeo I fell asleep but woke up to find your side of the bed empty, why?" She asked.

"My bad, but you know I'm out there tryna tie up loose ends," Shyne answered kissing her forehead.

"You could have called. You know I worry about you," Kendra said sitting up.

"I know and it won't happen again, I promise," he smiled.

Kendra never understood how any female could get used to living like this. She knew how the game was and even though Shyne was well respected in the streets, there was always someone wanting what he had. Who would do anything to get it. Now days no one was loyal money was the rout to all evil. Everybody was out tryna survive just like the next.

"Baby, listen, don't worry about me. Whatever's meant to happen it will happen good or bad," Shyne said kissing Kendra on the lips.

"How can you say not to worry about you?"

"I don't mean it like that. I'm not out there wildin' out like back in the day. As of lately, I've been tying up loose ends tryna leave that shit alone. I found something, well someone else to keep my attention," Shyne answered squeezing her tight.

"Nae is on her way over," Kendra said.

"Is everything okay?" Shyne asked.

"I don't know," Kendra answered as she got up throwing on one of Shyne's tank tops and a pair of his basketball shorts. While she got dress Shyne went into the closet grabbed two of his guns. He knew if Nae was on her way so was Kash.

They made their way downstairs as they continued talking.

There was a knock at the door. Shyne answered.

"Where are my babies?" Nae asked looking from Shyne to Kendra.

"They are upstairs sleep," Kendra answered. They watched as Nae ran upstairs.

"What's goin' on?" Shyne asked looking at Kash who was walking in.

"She had a dream about that nigga, Meccah. She said the nigga killed me and my kids," Kash sighed.

"What?" Kendra asked as she rushed upstairs to check on Nae.

"I'm taking that nigga out tonight," Kash said.

"Fuck is we waiting on? Let's roll out," Shyne said tapping his waist.

"Let's go," Kash said as he turned to walk out the door, Shyne right behind him.

*

Kendra stood at the door watched as Nae bear hugged her babies while she cried and rocked them back and forth. She wanted to talk to Nae but she would let her have her moment. She turned to walk away.

"Ken, it felt so surreal," Nae spoke. "I mean I stood there watching him kill my babies and Kash," she said wiping the tears away. It was no use because the more she wiped tears away the more they fell.

"Nae you and Kash need to make up y'all minds. It isn't just about you two anymore," Kendra said stepping back into the room. "You know niggas and bitches will do anything to see you fall. Now days nobody wanna see anybody happy," Kendra said.

"I know, I'm starting to regret moving back to Cali," Nae said.

"I don't think it was Cali. It doesn't matter where you two moved the drama and bullshit was sure to unfold," Kendra said. "Nae you remember how we promised we would never give a nigga our hearts again?"

Nae laughed. "Do I? That was my motto until I met Kash ass. He changed all that." She said.

"Right here we are back at it again. Only difference this time is, I think this go round its real," Kendra said.

Before Nae decided to move up North she and Kendra were thick as thieves. They ran with the hustlers getting money with them. They had done the one thing they said they wasn't and fell for the niggas they were working for. Just as always everything seemed so promising in the beginning, but when niggas start making a dollar over lunch money they wanna change up and front for the bitches that would have never talked to them before the icy chains and flashy cars came into play. For the two of them money was never the problem because they would do whatever it took to get what they needed. If that meant hustlering or busting their asses on a 9-5, they were getting it, never depending on a nigga for anything.

"Whatever happened to Dame and Dime?" Nae asked.

"Girl, a year after you left, Dame found out the bitch he left you for had HIV," Kendra answered.

"For real?" Nae asked. Kendra nodded her head yes.

"Soon after that he found out she had passed it on to him. He killed the bitch before killin' himself," she said.

"Wow," Nae said shocked.

"As for Dime, I don't know whatever happened to him. After his brother died it was as if he just disappeared," Kendra said shrugging her shoulders.

Nae grabbed her ringing phone. "Hello?" She answered.

"Where are you?" Dani asked.

"Home, why where am I supposed to be?" Nae asked.

"Bitch, everyone's her but you, Kash, Kendra, and Shyne," Dani said.

"Everyone's where?" Nae asked.

"Jamaica, we're waiting for y'all," she answered.

"Fuck!" Nae said. "I'm sorry, I forgot, but we will be on the plane in the morning," Nae assured. She had totally forgotten about the email she had received from Ray and Brandi about the trip to Jamaica.

"Good, cause he said he isn't doin' nothing until y'all get here," Dani said.

"Ok, we'll be there some time tomorrow," Nae said before hanging up.

"Is everything good?" Kendra asked.

"Yeah, we are out to Jamaica in the morning," answered Nae.

"Vacation?"

"Something like that Jacques is goin' to propose to Cherry and he wants us all there," Nae said.

"Aww shit, that's what's up," Kendra said. "I'm gonna go get some sleep." She said getting up. Nae nodded her understanding as she continued holding her babies close.

She was pissed with herself for forgetting all about the Jamaica trip. She thanked god for it. She needed to get away and clear her mind. Nae wanted nothing more than to get her babies out of harm's way. She didn't trust Meccah and wasn't gonna put anything pass him.

*

"What's the deal?" Shyne asked as him and Kash drove around.

"I'm waiting on a call now. I have no choice but to take this nigga out," Kash answered. "I don't put anything pass any nigga."

"That's understandable, but what call are you waiting for?" Shyne asked.

"He home addresses," answered Kash.

"No need. I know where that nigga be at all times," Shyne said directing Kash to Meccah.

Ten minutes later they were pulling up in front of a club.

"What are we doin' here?" Kash asked looking from the club to Shyne.

"You want Meccah? Well he's in there," Shyne assured.

"How do you know?"

"Because I know how the nigga moves," answered Shyne. "Don't believe me? Go inside."

"I believe you," Kash said as he parked the car and waited. He tapped his finger on the steering wheel as he got lost in his thoughts.

Kash didn't know how long he and Shyne had been sitting in front of the club waiting for Meccah to exit.

*

Meccah stumbled out of the club with a bitch draped under his arm. Unaware of the danger he was in. He didn't care about shit other than getting home and jumping into some pussy. His stunning had paid off like he felt it should have. He had spent way more money than he had planned but that was a small price to pay for some pussy.

Nae had crossed his mind a few times throughout the night but he refuse to play second to anyone. He was smart enough to know when to say fuck it and move it. The only problem with that was, he was a young street nigga tryna build up his reputation, so backing down from Kash and Shyne was something he couldn't do.

Kash hadn't been in the game for years but it didn't matter who Meccah asked around town. Niggas seem to know his name, only pissing him off that much more. Making him more determined to take him out, a young nigga like

Meccah taking a street legend out would sure boost his reputation and his already big ego up a few notches.

Meccah would never get the chance to figure Kash out. He had followed him a few times tryna learn how he moved. But like most street niggas, Kash routines were always different. He never took the same way home twice, he never stayed in one place to long, and he seem to always know what was going on around him at all time.

"Now that's what you call a smart street nigga." Meccah thought with a slight smile on his face. He had wondered a time or two how things would have been if he and Kash met on different terms. That too was a question he would never get an answer to.

"Meccah, are you alright?" The girl asked as he leaned against a parked car.

"Hell no my head spinning like a mothafucka right now," he said as he closed his eyes. Everything around him was spinning; he knew he was in no shape to drive anywhere. He hoped he stayed up long enough to get some pussy.

"I'll drive," she said holding her hands out for his car keys. Meccah reached into his pocket for them handing them to her. She stood him up to help him the rest of the way to his car.

"Y'all look like y'all can use some help," they heard a voice from behind say.

"We are fine, thanks," she said as she struggled with Meccah heavy body.

"Shawty, I advise you to leave while you still can," Kash

said as he approached helping her stand Meccah to his feet. The woman looked up, from the tone of his voice she could tell he meant business. She was just pissed that her plans to rob Meccah wasn't gonna work out after all. She sucked her teeth and rolled her eyes as she walked off.

Shyne laughed, he knew why she was so pissed. "Shawty, empty his pockets. Where he's goin', money isn't accepted." She stopped turning to face him to see if he was serious. Meccah nodded his head to assure her that he was. She smiled as she rushed back over to Meccah reaching into his pockets. She pulled out everything he had to offer including his wallet.

"Bitch, you were planning to rob me?" Meccah asked grilling her.

She laughed. "I just did, thanks," she said as she waved the bills she had just taken from his pocket. "Me robbing you should be the least of your worries," she said finally walking off.

"Fuck y'all pussy ass niggas," Meccah spat as he tried his best to stand to his feet. He wasn't about to beg for his life, he was going out standing on his toes.

"Bruh, you know you can't body him right here?" Shyne asked looking around at all the drunken party goers that were still leaving the club. Kash knew that, but at this point he didn't give a fuck as long as the nigga was dead before the sun was up.

Kash grabbed Meccah pulling him down the block. He half carried and half dragged him around the corner as Shyne followed close behind.

Meccah knew this was the end of the road for him. He had made his bed and now it was time for him to lay in it.

Kash turned the corner dropping Meccah face first into the ground. Meccah tried to get up but he couldn't. "Didn't I tell you you were just another nigga who wanted what I had? And didn't I tell you I was gonna come out on top?" Kash asked. "I always do. And didn't I tell you, Nae will always be mine, No matter what we go through?" He asked pulling his gun from his waist line.

"Suck my dick!" Meccah spat as he tried spitting on Kash, but it missed by a few inches.

Kash laughed as he sat Meccah up, leaning him against the building. "Suck on this, nigga," Kash said as he shoved the barrow of his gun down Meccah's throat. He forced the gun in his mouth breaking his top two front teeth before pulling the trigger. Kash and Meccah watched as Meccah's brain matter painted the wall behind him as his body slowly slid to the side. Kash stood there staring at Meccah's dead body as if he was in a trance.

"Bruh, we gotta go," Shyne said as he looked around.

Kash tucked his gun away and slowly walked away.

Killing Meccah was something he knew he had to do. There was no way around that. Just like he knew finding and killing Maria was something that had to be done as well.

Shyne and Kash jumped back into the car leaving the scene with the rest of the drunken party goers as if nothing had just happened.

*

The first couple of minutes of the ride were quiet, until Shyne spoke.

"Are you alright?"

"I'm straight, just sick and tired of all the bullshit that goes on in my life," answered Kash.

"The only way things will change is if you change the shit you be doin'," Shyne said. "You can't expect change if you're still out here doin' the same shit."

Kash knew Shyne was right. But he felt he had changed for the better. For starters he wasn't in the game anymore and hasn't been in a few years. He wasn't out fuckin' bitches like he had been when he was younger. All he was trying to do was keep the one woman who captured his heart happy. When she was happy so was he.

"You still have a chance to make it up to your lady. If it was over she wouldn't still be around," Shyne said.

The rest of the way to Kendra crib, Kash thought on what Shyne had said.

*

Shyne and Kash entered the house to find it quiet, letting them know that everyone had fallen asleep. Shyne made his way up to the bedroom leaving Kash on his own.

Kash walked into the kitchen to find him a drink. He was so deep into his thoughts that he never heard when Nae walked into the kitchen behind him.

"What did you do?" She asked getting his attention.

"I did what I had to do," he answered looking at her. Nae ran up to him wrapping her arms around his neck tightly.

It didn't matter how hard she tried or how many times she said it was over, she couldn't. They shared a bond like no other. Kash was the only man, Nae let capture her entire heart and he wouldn't let go or give it back. She knew death was the only thing that would ever break them apart. But it would never taint their love for each other.

Nae felt there wasn't any need to ask Kash of what happened. What was done was done and she couldn't change that. She was just happy that he walked back thru that door, back to her.

"We are leaving for Jamaica in the morning," Nae said.

"Why?"

"Jacques wants us out there," answered Nae. "Everyone is there but us."

"That's cool," Kash said. Wondering what Jacques had planned. He had been so wrapped up in all his problems that he barely talked to any of his niggas as much as he use too. "We can use this little get away," Kash said pouring a drink.

Nae looked into Kash handsome face and smiled. "You know I love you right?" She asked.

"I know and I love you too," replied Kash.

"Will you always love me?" Nae asked. Kash looked at her with a frown on his face.

"Always," he answered.

"You promise?"

"Yes," Kash said.

Nae leaned up to kiss him on his lips before she turned leaving him standing in the kitchen alone. She went to snuggle with her babies. After the dream she had, she wanted to just hold her babies close. She was happy Meccah was no longer a problem. She knew that didn't mean they were in the clear. Nae didn't know how many times her and Kash relationship would be tested, all she knew was that he was the love of her life and couldn't see herself living without him.

Chapter Sixteen

JJ and Jewel were sitting downstairs watching TV when they heard cars pulling up. They both jumped up running to the windows. They didn't speak as they watched to see who would get out of the two cars pulling up.

"Daddy, Auntie Ray is here!" JJ yelled, as him and Jewel ran to meet them at the front door.

"Who's here?" Cherry asked following them to the door. "Oh shit, what are y'all doin' here?" She asked seeing her girls approaching. She went down the line giving all her girls hugs.

"You know it wouldn't be a party without us," Nija said.

"Shit I came to see what Jamaica has to offer and to see what they weed be like," Vonne laughed dead serious.

"All my uncles are here!" Jewel said. "Did y'all bring me anything?" She asked with a smile on her face.

King picked her up. "Can I get a hug first?" He asked throwing her in the air. She giggled as she wrapped her arms around his neck.

"She already acts just like her damn mother and aunts," Melo said shaking his head.

"Well did you bring me anything?" Jewel asked looking at King. "Uncle Melo, what about you?" She asked. "Never mind, I'm going to talk to uncle Chase, Rell, and Jason. I know they got me something," Jewel said as she got down.

"Ain't that about a bitch?" King laughed. "What up, JJ?" He asked giving him a pound. JJ punched him in his stomach before running off. JJ stopped in his tracks. "Y'all not seeing my hands," he said before taking off.

"What the fuck?!" King said.

"My lil' nigga got a mean right jab don't he?" Jacques asked laughing as he finally came into view. "I taught him well. What up with y'all niggas?" He asked as he gave each of his niggas a pound and brotherly hug.

"The question is why that hell you got us flying across the world?" Jason asked.

"I got a surprise for my baby and I wanted y'all niggas to be here for it," Ques answered as they walked further into the house.

"What surprise?" Rell asked.

"Ayo, Ray!" Jacques called out.

"Where's the weed at, nigga?" Chase asked taking a seat.

"What's up?" Ray asked walking into the room.

"You got that for me?" Jacques asked.

"Yeah, hold up, let me go grab it," she said rushing out of the room.

"Got what?" Melo asked. No one knew what was going on but Ray and her girls.

Ray walked back in handing Jacques the small ring box. Jacques opened the box to admire the ring. "Yo this shit fire," he smiled.

"Let us see," King said sitting up in his seat.

Jacques passed the ring off.

"Jacques, it's a natural fancy blue marquise diamond ring featuring a magnificent 2.44 CT GIA certified also has grey blue, internally flawless marqueise diamond surrounded by pave set white and pink diamonds," Ray said. "It's mounted in 18k white and rose gold." She finished.

"Damn!" Rell whistled.

"How much that run a nigga for?" Jason asked.

"Price isn't the issue," answered Jacques.

"I take it you like it?" Ray asked.

"Yeah," Ques nodded his head as he admired the ring once again. "Only thing is, I hope, Cherry likes it."

"She will love it, but if she don't I got dib's on it," Ray laughed but was dead serious.

"Congrats," King said dapping Jacques up.

"Thanks, man it's about that time. She been rocking with ya boy for a while now. It's only right I make her my wife," Jacques said closing the ring box and putting it in his pocket.

"What's up with Kash? Rell asked.

"I can't answer that I haven't talk to him since I've been here," answer Ques.

"Kash is handling his business. He called me the night before we flew down asking for some information on some nigga name, Meccah," Chase answered. "He never went into details about what was goin' on; he just said he'll holla at me about it later."

*

The ladies sat around the kitchen catching up.

"Mommy, that isn't fair, my uncles didn't bring me anything," Jewel pouted.

"Jewel, they aren't gonna buy you something every time they see you," Cherry said.

"Why not? If they miss me they will," Jewel said.

"That's right, make 'em come outta their pockets," Vonne laughed.

Cherry waved Vonne off as she removed Jewel from the counter. "Go find your brother and play," Cherry said to Jewel.

"But I wanna talk to my aunties," Jewel pouted.

"Jewel go play," Cherry said. Jewel rolled her eyes and stormed out of the kitchen.

"Keep playing with me and see if I don't whoop ya ass," Cherry called after her.

"That girl is gonna be a problem," Nija laughed.

"She's already a problem," Cherry said shaking her head.

"Ladies, we can finish this chat as we shop," Nija said on her way out the kitchen.

"Hold up, where's Nae?" Vonne asked.

"I called her," Dani said. They should be here sometime today or tonight. They caught their flight this morning."

They all left the kitchen to wash and change their clothes.

Brandi stopped in the living room where the niggas was. "Jacques, what time should we have her back?" She asked.

"In about two hours," he answered checking his watch.

"Shit, I'll see if I can make that happen," Brandi said walking off.

"What was the point in you asking me if you aren't gonna have her back when I ask?" Jacques asked looking at Brandi.

"My fault, but I just thought about it. We are gonna need way more than two hours shopping," she laughed.

"Ayo, make sure y'all asses snatch Nae something up to wear tonight," he called after her. He knew Nae was goin' to be pissed about not being able to shop with the rest of the girls.

Ten minutes later the ladies were rushing out the door ready to spend money. They stopped in the living to get some money from the men.

"Baby, I'm gonna need that black card of yours," Ray said.

Melo reached into his pocket for his wallet, without asking any questions. The rest of the fellas did the same.

"See this is why I love you," Dani said as she kissed King.

"We have our own money but y'all let us spend yours," Vonne laughed. "This is the life to live."

"We are in Jamaica, enjoy yourself, ma," Rell said to Nija.

"Baby, believe me I'm gonna enjoy myself to the fullest," she smiled taking his card from his hand.

"Brandi, make sure you bring me something I can take off you tonight," Chase winked.

"I got you, babe," Brandi laughed.

Jacques didn't say anything as he passed Cherry his wallet. "Ma, everything's on me," he finally said. Cherry kissed him smiling.

"You know I love you right?" She asked.

"You can show me how much tonight," Jacques replied.

"Can y'all do that shit in private?" Vonne asked.

"Mommy, can I go shopping with you and my Aunties?" Jewel asked.

"Come on," Cherry laughed as she picked Jewel up.

"Two hours," Jacques said. "JJ, you hanging with me and these niggas here," he said looking at his son.

"Are we going to play the game?" JJ asked.

"You got money?" Melo asked. JJ nodded his head as he reached into his pocket.

"Daddy said to always keep money on me. Because I never know what will happen," he said showing the one hundred dollar bill he had.

Everyone laughed.

"It's the truth. I can't have my lil' nigga with empty pockets," Jacques said.

"Daddy, I need some new J's. Mine got messed up," JJ said as he grabbed the game controller.

"I got you," laughed Jacques. He made sure his son and daughter stayed fly. It was only right.

*

Nae looked out the window as the car came to a complete stop. It had been a long plane right but she was too excited about seeing her girls. She would sleep when she got the chance.

"Babe, are we staying here?" Nae asked as she looked over at Kash. He had a smile sitting on his face. He loved when Nae called him babe. The way it rolled off her tongue was sexy as hell.

"Yeah," answered Kash as he climbed out of the car. He walked around to open the door for Nae who was holding Keikeo in her arms. Both Keikeo and Lanaya were knocked out. The driver got out of the car to help Nae and Kash with their bags.

Nae didn't wait for Kash as she went and knocked on the door.

"Thanks, you can just sit the bags by the door and I got it from there," Kash said as he tipped the driver. The driver unloaded the trunk before getting back in his car pulling off.

Nae opened the door and was hit with a cloud of smoke. *"Right on time."* She thought.

"Hello?" Nae called out as she walked into the house.

"Aww shit," Chase said as he walked out of the kitchen. Nae flipped him off while rolling her eyes. "What's good with you?" He asked giving her a hug.

"Not much, but you can take your nephew and lay him down," she said handing Keikeo to him.

"Nah, his little ass gotta get up," Chase said as he gave Kash a pound.

"Where are my bitches?" Nae asked as she walked into the living room where, King, Jacques, Rell, Melo, and JJ were sitting with their eyes glued to the TV.

"They went shopping," Jacques answered.

"Really, so that means I'm stuck here with you all until they get back?" Nae asked pissed.

"Yep," Rell laughed holding a blunt out for her. Nae snatched it from his hand.

JJ!" Nae said as she passed the blunt so that she could give him a hug.

"Hi auntie, I can't talk right now," he said never looking at her or attempting to give her a hug.

Nae shook her head as she wrapped her arms around him anyways.

"Now that the gangs all here we can get this shit under way," Jacques said standing up.

"Let me see the ring," Nae said.

Jacques reached into his pocket pulling out the ring box. He let Nae open it herself. "Where is Kendra and Shyne?" He asked.

"Shyne wanted to keep Kendra all to himself," answered Nae. "Aye, this shit tough," she said admiring the ring. "Congrats," she said giving him a hug.

"Thanks," replied Jacques.

There was a knock at the door. Jacques walked to answer it. It was the caters he had ordered for this special day.

"This shit is mean, though," Kash said looking at the ring.

"Come on, fuck y'all thought I was gonna come half stepping?" Jacques asked walking back into the room. He took the ring from Nae hands placing it back into this pocket.

Nae pushed him.

"Here's the deal. We are gonna all eat dinner outside on the beach, and chill over some drinks. No bullshit," Ques said pointing to everyone in the room. "And as the sun is setting is when I'm gonna pop the question to my baby," he informed everyone.

Nae jumped up and down screaming.

"Aye, Kash, do I gotta put her ass in a strait jacket?" Ques asked.

"Fuck you nigga," Nae laughed. "I'm just juiced about my girl getting engaged," Nae said. "I'm 'bout to go wash my ass," Nae informed everyone.

She couldn't wait to see the look on Cherry's face.

*

The girls arrived almost an hour late but Jacques wasn't gonna let that fuck up his picture perfect night. When they saw Nae they all almost forgot about dinner.

"Ayo, y'all can talk at the table," Melo said. "Go get dress," he said shutting their excitement down.

"These niggas sure do know how to fuck up a bitch mood," Vonne said.

"We do have to get ready," Nija said.

"True, we are already late," Brandi laughed. "It wasn't my fault," she made sure to say.

"Why are we getting dressed for dinner?" Cherry asked.

"Girl, come on," Ray said as they all headed upstairs.

"Man, are you ready?" Rell asked.

"Ready as I'll ever be. But this is something I gotta do. I love the hell out of that girl," Jacques answered as he watched Jewel, Lanaya, Keikeo, and JJ running around on the beach.

"It's the right thing to do, too," Jason said walking up. "Lil' ma been holding things down for you since y'all be together," he said. Rell agreed.

"Indeed," Jacques smiled.

*

Everyone was laughing and joking while they ate dinner and enjoy themselves. This was the first time in a while that they were all together and no one was arguing or fighting. That's just how Jacques wanted it to be.

"I got a question," Vonne said.

Everyone looked at her. Because they all knew some ill shit was about to come out her mouth.

"Ok, I have a couple questions," she laughed. "One: who's cleaning this shit up and Two: where the weed at?" She asked smiling.

"Shut up," they all laughed throwing napkins at her.

"Aye, watch the face and hair," she said making sure nothing touched her face or got into her hair.

"Somebody turn some music on," Brandi said.

Rell got up to turn the radio on. Adorn by Miguel spilled from the speakers. Every male grabbed their other half pulling them close singing along with Miguel.

It was truly a picture perfect moment that none of them wanted to end.

As the song came to an end, Jacques grabbed, Cherry pulling her towards the water.

"Where are we goin'? She asked laughing.

"I wanna holla at you alone for a little while," answered

Jacques. Cherry didn't fight or argue with him as they walked to the water hand in hand.

"Are you enjoying yourself?" He asked as he wrapped his arms around her waist as they looked at the sun setting. It was a pretty sight.

"I am and I wanna thank you for it," Cherry said.

"Ma, you know you don't have to thank me for anything. The things I'm doin' I'm supposed to be doin' as your man," Jacques said.

"And you're doin' a hell of a job," Cherry said causing Jacques to smile.

Jacques removed his arms from around her waist as he kissed her neck.

"Cherry," Jacques begin as he got down on one knee behind her. "You say you love me and you know I love you with everything in me. I know we've had our share of ups and down but I can't see myself living without you," Jacques said. "And I don't plan on living without you. What I'm saying is will you marry me?" He asked.

"What did you just say?" Cherry asked turning around to find him on a bended knee.

It wasn't that she didn't hear him; she just wanted to make sure she heard him right the first time. Jacques laughed.

"I said will you marry me?" He repeated holding the ring box up to her face.

"You really mean that shit?" Cherry asked holding back her tears.

"Yes, now will you answer the question?" Jacques laughed.

"Yes, baby, I will," Cherry answered as she wrapped her arms around his neck. Not giving him a chance to slide the ring on her finger.

"Damn girl!" Jacques said as he fell backwards into the sand. "Can I at least place the ring on your finger?" He asked causing Cherry to laugh through her teary eyes.

Jacques placed the ring on her finger as Cherry placed kisses all over his face.

"I love you, nigga!" Cherry laughed.

"Thank god!" Ques joked as Cherry finally let him up.

Her girls all screamed Congratulations from where they stood.

"Y'all asses knew about this didn't y'all?" She asked as her and Ques walked back to the house.

"We did," Brandi laughed.

"Let us see that ring on your finger," Dani said.

Cherry wiggled her hand in their faces as they all admired the ring together.

The party had just begun to get underway as they continued to enjoy each other's company.

Chapter Seventeen

Maria stepped outside of the hospital looking around. It had been six long months that she was trapped inside; healing from the beat down Nae had put on her. She had suffered with two broken ribs, a broken arm, and a collapsed lung. It pained her even more knowing that she couldn't make it to her father's funeral, only putting an even more bitter taste in her mouth. The entire time she was laid up in the hospital all she could think about was revenge. She finally had a plan to end it all. Nae never lied when she said she wanted Maria to wish she was dead. The pain she had gone thru was nothing she had experienced before and most days she wanted nothing more than to just give up. But revenge was what kept her going.

The element of surprise was what she was going for. Maria knew she couldn't underestimate Nae or Kash. She had done that a time or two in her life and every time she did, it backfired on her. This time she was gonna come out on top, shining.

Did she still have strong feeling for Kash? Yes, but as of now she loved and hated him at the same damn time. It didn't matter how hard she tried to stay away from him, she couldn't. Not even the fact that he killed her father. A single tear fell from her left eye. She quickly wiped it away before a river could start. Crying wasn't something she often did and she wasn't about to start now.

Kash had taken one of the most important people from her and it was only right she did the same. Maria had battled with her heart and head for the last six months.

Her head was telling her to leave well enough alone but her heart wanted revenge. She knew she would never be with Kash; she had come to that conclusion a long time ago. Maria felt if he couldn't be happy with her, he shouldn't be happen with anyone else.

Maria watched as the cab came to a complete stop in front of her before she stepped up, opening the back door sliding inside. She sat there for a while thinking of what she wanted to do. She finally gave the cabdriver her destination. She made herself comfortable because she knew she was gonna be sitting there for a while.

Maria didn't know which hurt more, her heart or her body. The fact that Kash didn't love her or see in her what he saw in Nae had always bothered her. All her life she had used her body to get any man she wanted and anything from them. But Kash was different, which is what made her go after him even more. It just so happened she had falling head over heels for him only to get played.

"You have played the game long enough. You have lost, leave it alone." Her mind threw at her. Maria shook her head no. She couldn't leave anything alone. She was already in too deep.

Maria was deep in thought; she didn't realize that the cab had come to a complete stop.

"Ma'am, we're here," the cabdriver said. She sat up in the back seat as she rolled down her window. She looked outside to find Kash, Nae, and their kids running around the yard with smiles on their faces. She frowned because she felt that was supposed to be her and not Nae. *"She stole my life."* Maria thought becoming even more pissed.

She didn't know she was crying until a tear rolled down her cheek. She wiped it away as she promised herself that she would have the last laugh.

"Let's go," she said never taking her eyes of Nae and Kash.

"Where to next?" The cabbie asked. Maria gave him her next destination as he slowly pulled off. Maria continued to keep her eyes glued to the happy family; she felt was supposed to be hers. When she couldn't see them anymore she sat back and sunk into the seat with her eyes closed.

*

Nae went into the house smiling. This was the first time in a while that she wore a smile on her face and Kash has put it there. For the last six months they had been taking one day at a time trying to rekindle what they have built. Both knew it wasn't gonna be easy but neither one could see themselves living without the other.

Nae knew they weren't in the clear just yet because Maria was still out there somewhere waiting to cause more drama in their lives.

"I have to find and kill that bitch." Nae thought knowing that that was the only way the madness would end.

"You okay?" Kash asked walking into the kitchen.

"Yeah I'm fine," Nae smiled. But Kash knew she was lying.

"Nae, don't lie to me what's on ya mind?" He asked taking a seat.

"I'm worried that Maria is out there plotting," answered

Nae. Kash sighed as he ran his hand over his face. He had been stressing about the same thing.

He had called Chase a while back to see if he could find any type of location on Maria but he came up empty.

"Let's not worry about that-"

"Kash, how can you say let's not worry about that? When she's the reason we're goin' thru this in the first place?" Nae asked.

"Listen, I have Chase searching for her now," replied Kash. "Are we gonna start arguing about this?" He asked.

"No, but I do have the right to worry. I don't want anything to happen to you, me, or our fuckin' kids," Nae said. "I should have killed the bitch when I had the chance," Nae mumbled.

"What did you say?" Kash asked.

"I said I should have killed that bitch when I had the chance," Nae repeated herself. "The day we got into it at the bar. Before I got there I found her parked outside watching our home. So I dragged her out her car and beat her with a crowbar. At the time I wanted her to wish she was dead. Now I regret not killing her ass," Nae said.

"Why are you just now tellin' me this?" Kash asked as he removed his phone from his pocket. He called Chase. Nae shrugged her shoulders.

"I didn't think we were gonna get back together." She answered

"Yo, I can't find that bitch nowhere," Chase said when he

answered his phone.

"Check all hospitals in the area. You might find her or it may give us a lead as to where she is," Kash said.

"Iight, I'll hit you back in a few," Chase said disconnecting the call.

"Mommy, can I and Keikeo have a juice please?" Lanaya said as she walked into the kitchen.

Nae walked over to the fridge grabbing two juice boxes. She opened both before handing them to Lanaya.

"Thank you!" She said as she skipped out of the kitchen.

"I don't know why you would think some shit like that," Kash said. Nae rolled her eyes.

"Tell me something good," Kash said answering his ringing phone.

"I finally got something for you. She was just released from the hospital today," Chase answered.

"Fuck!" Kash said. "Is there any way you can trace her phone?" He asked.

"I've tried that as of now it's off. But as soon as she turns it on, I will be able to," answered Chase.

"Good lookin' out. Keep me posted," Kash said disconnecting the call.

"What's wrong?" Nae asked.

"She was just released from the hospital today," he told her. "But as of now Chase, can't trace her phone because it's off." He said.

"Don't you dare come out your mouth to tell me I have to leave my home," Nae said reading Kash like a book. "Because I'm not," she finished.

"Nae, I need you and my kids out of harm's way," Kash tried to reason.

"We can send the kids to Lisa if we have too but I am not goin' anywhere," Nae spat. "We supposed to be in this together, remember?"

Kash sighed; he knew there was no use in arguing with Nae about leaving. Her mind was made up.

"Kash, I will not let her run me off," Nae said. "The only way I'm goin' out is on my own two feet. Won't any bitch be able to say she ran me away from anything."

"Whatever," Kash said walking away. Not wanting to argue. But something in his gut was telling him to stay there and argue with Nae until she agreed to leave. He just hoped he wouldn't regret it later down the line.

Nae didn't understand what the problem was about her not wanting to run from a bitch that didn't understand that she wasn't wanted and never will be wanted. She had dealt with dangerous people worse than Maria.

*

The first thing Maria did was take a nice relaxing bath when she got home. She didn't have anything else to do or anyone to call or talk to. The only person she ever had in her corner was her father and because she didn't leave the bullshit alone with Kash, he was dead.

All though she had been thinking of the many things she was going to do to Nae, her mind always had her second guessing herself. One day she was sure of what she wanted to do and other days she didn't think it was such a good idea. Maria couldn't live with the fact that Kash no longer wanted her. *"He never wanted you."* Her mind threw out at her. She sighed because she knew it was nothing but the truth. It didn't matter how many times over the last few months, she told herself she was revenging her father's death, she knew that was far from the truth.

Maria sat there fighting with herself on whether or not to call Kash. It had been so long since she had heard his voice or was in close range with him. Seeing him earlier that day only caused her mind to mess with her ever more. Before Maria knew what she was doing. She had her phone in her hands dialing, Kash number. *"I just want to hear his voice."* She thought.

*

Kash stood at the backdoor watching Keikeo and Lanaya run around playing. The sounds of their playful voices eased his racing mind and pounding heart. When he was around them nothing else really mattered. They made the biggest impact on his life. Kash looked at having kids as a blessing and a curse, for many different reasons. Kash knew there was no such thing as raising your kids the right way. They would eventually venture off into the world on their own, and they would also have to learn from their own mistakes. He never wanted his kids to suffer from the mistakes he had made.

Kash grabbed his cell not bothering to check the caller ID.

"Hello?" He said into the phone. He didn't get a responds. He removed the phone from his ear looking at the screen to see if someone was still on his line. "Why must you play on my phone?" He asked with a slight attitude.

Kash listened hoping whoever it was would say what they wanted and stopped playing on his phone. Than he thought about it, the only person to ever play on his phone was, Maria.

He headed for the kitchen for Nae's cell phone. He needed to see if Chase could trace the call. Kash didn't have enough time because before he made it to the kitchen the line went dead. He sighed deeply as he called Chase once again.

"Is everything alright with you?" Nae asked knowing something had just pissed him off.

"No, she just called my fuckin' phone," answered Kash.

Nae didn't need to ask who but she did anyways.

"Who called your phone?" She asked looking at him.

"Maria, I know it was her. It had to be. She's the only one that would call me private and not say anything," Kash said. "I need to find her like now."

Nae knew nothing good was gonna come out of Maria calling and playing on Kash phone. She knew for a fact that she was back and was planning on finishing what she started.

*

Maria sat there with a smile on her face. Kash still sound good as usually. She had half the mind to say something but she didn't, only because she knew they would be talking to each other real soon.

Chapter Eighteen

Cherry nervously rushed around the shop making sure everything was how it should be. She would finally be opening for business and she wanted everything perfect.

"Ma, relax," Jacques said pulling her close.

"I can't, baby, I'm nervous. I don't want anything to go wrong," Cherry said looking around once more.

"Babe, everything is gonna be fine. Stop stressing," Jacques said kissing her lips.

Since they had returned from Jamaica six months ago everything had been great for the too. The drama wasn't over but that didn't stop Cherry from finally getting her project up and running. Anna was still a big issue but neither of them had heard from her or about her in six months. Did that stop them from worrying about her or wondering what she had planned? No, they just didn't let it affect them or their lives. They knew when it was time to face her they would be ready and waiting. Neither of them knew when that time would be.

Cherry cell phone rang scaring the shit out of her. She damn near jumped out of her skin.

"Relax," Jacques demanded this time as Cherry answered her phone.

"Hello?" She answered not bothering to check the caller ID.

"Congratulations," Anna said on the other end of the

phone. "Did you miss me?" She laughed.

"Bitch, what do you want?" Cherry asked in a hushed tone.

"I just wanted to congratulate you being that this will be your last happy day," Anna said. Cherry laughed.

"I see you're still playing games, games you clearly will never win," Cherry said.

Anna laughed, "Cherry, we will see soon enough who will win this game, good luck."

"Luck is something I never needed. You should be wishing yourself luck," Cherry said.

"I survived this long without it," Anna chuckled.

"Fuck off my line, bitch," Cherry spat before disconnecting the call. She took a deep breath before releasing it. She wasn't about to let Anna of all people fuck up her big day.

"Vonne, has finally stepped in the mothafuckin' building!" Vonne said as she made her way inside. "I'm always ready for the cameras, where they at?" She asked.

Cherry laughed, she was more than happy to see her girls.

"This bitch," Nae said shoving Vonne out the way.

"Hating does not look good on you," Vonne said as she playfully rolled her eyes.

"Cherry, you have outdone yourself," Nija said looking around.

"Are you excited?" Brandi asked.

"Congrats," Ray said.

"Vonne, I see your ass is still full of yourself," Cherry laughed. "Thanks, I'm more nervous but very much excited," she said.

"Of course, if I don't love me who will?" Vonne asked smiling. They all shook their heads. Cherry took her girls in. They all were dressed to impress as always.

Cherry loved her girls, no matter what they were doing or what was going on in their personal lives they always made time for each other. Supporting and showing love, what more can you ask for?

"You bitches rock," Cherry said.

"Cherry, what time are you opening?" Dani asked as she looked out the window. The line of people waiting to get inside was getting longer and longer as time passed.

"Umm in about thirty minutes, I wanted to spend some time with you guys first," answered Cherry.

"Damn! Y'all gotta check this bad bitch out," Vonne said looking at the pictures on the wall. "She's a bad bitch and she's working the hell out of that dress." She said.

All her girls walked over to see who she was talking about.

Ray sucked her teeth. "Bitch, you are too full of yourself," Ray said shoving her this time.

Vonne laughed again. "Y'all can't lie, I look damn good. Aye, y'all asses look almost as good as me."

"If you don't sit ya ass down," Brandi laughed.

"A'ight, I'm gonna chill," Vonne said taking a seat.

"Y'all remember that day?" Dani asked. "That was the first photo shoot we had ever done."

"Nija laughed, "We couldn't agree on anything, from the dresses down to the shoes."

"Hell yeah I remember that. Vonne and Nae asses was tryna hog the damn cameras," Brandi laughed.

"What?" Nae asked laughing. "No I wasn't. Okay I was only because this bitch wanted to shoot all to herself," she said pointing to Vonne.

"It ain't my fault the cameras love me. Hell I worked them mothafuckin' camera and it has paid off," Vonne said taking up for herself.

"That it did," Nija agreed.

"Cherry, what made you wanna open a modeling agency?" Kendra asked.

"I love fashion and it's something I've always wanted to do but couldn't because of the life style I chose," Cherry answered shrugging her shoulders. "This way I get to kill two birds with one stone. I design my own clothes and teach young girls in the A how to model all at once."

"Cherry, why you never said anything? You know Vonne and I could have plugged you in with a lot of big names," Nija said.

"You know I like to do things myself. The only thing they can do for me is give me sound advice," Cherry answered.

"I don't mean to break y'all little conversation up but it's time," Jacques said as he approached them.

"I hope you don't mind but Nija and I invited a few well known people we know to come check you out," Vonne said getting up from her seat.

"Yeah, we heard you were putting on a little fashion show, staring your own designs," Nija smiled.

"Oh gosh, y'all didn't?" Cherry said becoming very nervous again.

"We did," Vonne said.

"Why are you nervous? I'm sure you did a hell of a job," Ray said.

"How did y'all know about me designing?" Cherry asked.

"We know everything," Brandi said.

"We have a little surprise for you as well," Nae said.

Jacques grabbed Cherry hand as he pulled her to the door. She looked out and smiled. There were many people standing outside waiting to get in.

"Are you ready?" He asked.

"Ready as I'll ever be," she answered ready to open for business.

Jacques let Cherry hand go as he gave her a little push for her to go ahead and open the doors. It took her a little minute but she finally unlocked the doors. All she could hear was people cheering and clapping, causing her to smile even more. If anybody was to ask her how she felt, she wouldn't be able to put it in words at the moment. Jacques handled her a pair of big scissors and she cut the red bow as cameras snapped picture after picture. The cheers continued as she took a step back letting everyone in.

Once everyone was inside, Cherry took the stage.

She let everyone settle down before she began speaking.

"I just want to thank everyone for taking the time out to come support me and my dreams. I have worked really hard on something I take pride in doing and I just hope you all will love it as much as I do. Thanks again and enjoy," she said before walking off the stage. Everyone clapped and cheered as the lights went dim. A few moments later they came back on as music begin to play softly in the background.

The first model took the stage followed by the next and so forth.

Cherry was so wrapped up in making sure all the models were where they was supposed to be and had what the needed that she never noticed her girls were all back there changing into one of her very own designs.

Cherry had been nervous in the beginning but that all had changed and turned into excitement. She still couldn't believe that she had finally opened her very own modeling agency. She had gone from a dope dealer/killing to a business woman. *"Now that's what you call a true boss bitch."* She thought laughing.

"Last walk ladies," Cherry said as she took a peek at the crowd. The looks she could see let her know she had done the damn thing.

"How are you feeling?" Jacques asked walking up behind her wrapping his arms around her.

"Pretty damn good," she answered.

"I got a surprise for you," he whispered in her ear.

"And what might that be?" She asked. Jacques walked her to the stage. Cherry gasped when she saw her girls take the stage one by one wearing her designs. "You're the one that told them?" She asked looking up at Jacques. He nodded his head up and down.

"And guess what?"

"What?"

"We didn't even have to pay them," he laughed.

"Shut up," laughed Cherry. "You are so damn stupid." She said pushing him.

"I'm proud of you. I knew you could do it," he said kissing her lips.

"I couldn't have done it without you," she said as she turned around to give him a kiss on the lips.

"Thank me later," he winked. "Go, they're waiting on you," he said as he released her.

Cherry took the stage to a standing ovation.

She walked the runway holding a mic in her hand. "Once again I would like to thank everyone for coming out and I can't forget to thank my girls. They truly surprised me when they took the stage. Just another added bonus," she laughed. "Feel free to help yourself to the refreshments, thanks!" Cherry said taking a bow before switching her ass off the stage.

*

Anna stood off in a dark corner admiring Cherry's work. She had to admit that she had skills and had outdone herself, from the design of the shop to the runway. Not to mention, her designs were damn good.

"To bad she isn't gonna live long enough to enjoy it." Anna thought as she sipped from the wine glass she was holding.

She felt a small hand tapping her leg. "Hey, I know you," Jewel said looking up at her. Anna nervously looked around as she smiled at the pretty little girl. *"Damn, she has the memory of an elephant."* Anna thought.

"This is my cousin, Lanaya," Jewel said pointing to Lanaya.

"Jewel, I don't like her," Lanaya said running off.

"Are you going to say hi to mommy and daddy?" Jewel asked.

"No, can you keep a secret?" Anna said. Jewel nodded her head up and down.

"Good, you can't tell anyone I was here," Anna said looking around once more.

She couldn't believe she was talking to a three year old. "Okay, can you do that for me?" Jewel nodded her head again.

"But why, is it because mommy doesn't like you? Oooohhh, I know why," Jewel said covering her face as she giggled.

"And why do I want to you to keep my secret?" Anna asked. She wanted to know just what the little girl was thinking.

"Because mommy beat you up," Jewel answered. Anna frowned at her answer.

Anna frown turned into a smile as she came up with a plan.

"Jewel, would you like to take a walk with me?" Anna asked.

"No, mommy and daddy said I'm not supposed to talk to strangers," answered Jewel as she skipped around Anna.

"But I'm not a stranger, you know me," Anna tried to reason.

"I have to go ask mommy first. But if I do that I will be telling you secret," Jewel said.

"Jewel, we are only goin' outside for a little while. Don't you wanna go outside?"

Anna tried to pick Jewel up but Jewel wiggled and squirmed from her grip. "No, put me down, mommy!" Jewel screamed at the top of her lungs.

"Shut up," Anna mumbled as she tried carrying Jewel away but was having problems in doing so.

"DADDYYYY!" Jewel screamed again. Anna put her hand

over Jewel's mouth to stop her from screaming. Jewel bit her causing Anna to drop her.

"Shit, her little as bit me," Anna said as she check her hand out.

"Mommy!" Anna heard Jewel scream. She knew she had to get out of there before Cherry or Jacques spotted her. She had worked too hard on her plan to kill Cherry for it to go up in smoke before she could put it in motion.

*

"Princess, what's the matter?" Jacques asked as he picked a crying Jewel up. Jewel wrapped her arms around Jacques and buried her face into his neck.

"I told her I could keep a secret," Jewel mumbled into his neck.

"Told who?" Jacques asked confused.

"She's going to be mad if I tell you. She said you and mommy weren't supposed to know she was here," answered Jewel.

"Baby girl, it's okay she isn't gonna be mad. Tell me who?" Jacques damn near pleaded.

"I don't know her name. The lady mommy beat up," Jewel said. Jacques frowned as he passed Jewel to Kash.

"Who is she talkin' about?" Kash asked.

"Fuckin' Anna, man," Jacques said as he rushed to the front door.

Jacques didn't wanna alarm anyone but he needed to try

and catch her before she could get away.

*

Anna made it out quickly, she bumped into someone.

"Watch where you are goin'!" Vonne yelled as she pushed Anna for bumping into her.

"Excuse me, I'm sorry. I didn't see anyone standing there," Anna said as she took a good look at Vonne.

"Next time watch where you're goin'," Vonne warned. "Is there a reason as to why you're lookin' at me like that?" She asked Anna.

"I'm sorry," Anna lied. Anna recognized Vonne from the many pictures sitting around Jacques and Cherry's home.

"A'ight, bitch poof be gone," Vonne said waving her along. Anna quickly turned away and rushed up the street.

Damn, that was close." Anna thought as she made it a safe distance's from the shop.

She couldn't believe how well Jewel mind worked. She remembered her as if she had seen her the day before. "I have got to stop playing it so close if I wanna win this game," she mumbled as she got into her car.

Jacques rushed out the door looking both ways.

"What's wrong with you?" Nija asked looking at Jacques funny.

"Did y'all see a female rushing out of here?" He asked. "Shit," he said. There was no use in asking Vonne or Nija because neither of them knew how Anna looked.

"Yeah why?" Vonne asked. "A bitch just bumped into me rushing from inside you know here or something?"

"Which way did she go?" Ques asked. Vonne and Nija pointed the way she went. Ques took off in search of her.

"Okay, what was that all about?" Nija asked.

"Hell if I know. But let's go find out. I know Cherry has answers," Vonne said as they headed back inside.

*

Cherry was livid as she packed back and forth. She couldn't believe Anna had the nerve to show up at her opening and try taking Jewel.

"Mommy, I think she's mad at me," Jewel said.

"Why is she mad at you?" Cherry asked as she stopped pacing the floor.

"Because I told her I know why she wanted me to keep her secret," Jewel said.

"What secret?" Nae asked.

"She didn't want me to tell mommy or daddy that she was here. Then I told her I knew why she wanted me to keep her secret," Jewel said.

"And why did she want you to keep her secret?" Ray asked.

"Because, mommy beat her up," answered Jewel.

Cherry hugged Jewel tightly. "Baby, are you okay?" Cherry asked. Jewel nodded her head up and down.

I'm already on it," Brandi said walking away.

"I knew this was coming," Cherry said as she paced the floor again.

"Cherry, don't let that bitch fuck your night up. We'll get that bitch," Nae assured.

"That bitch tried to kidnap my fuckin' baby," Cherry said trying her hardest not to cry. "Oh god, where is JJ?" She asked in a panic.

"He's okay. Him and Keikeo are with the guys," Nija answered as her and Vonne walked into Cherry's office.

"I'm pissed I didn't know who that bitch was. I would have dragged her ass," Vonne said taking a seat.

"You saw her?" Cherry asked.

"Yeah, as she rushed out she bumped into me and had the nerve to look me up and down," Vonne answered. "Tuh, do you believe the nerve of that bitch?"

"Why didn't you tell us about this?" Dani asked.

"There really wasn't anything to tell. The bitch isn't really about that life. All she did was fuck up my cars and sneak into my home," answered Cherry.

"And that isn't something to tell?" Ray asked.

"I didn't think so," Cherry said. "That last time she did anything was before Ques and I left for Jamaica. Up until this point, we haven't heard or saw her. But I knew she would be back around."

Nae sighed deeply as she took a seat as well.

"You and Kash are still having problems?" Dani asked Nae.

"We are gonna always have problems as long as Maria is alive," Nae said.

"So, you too just don't tell us anything anymore?" Ray asked.

"It isn't like that," Nae said. "Why bother y'all with my issues when you all are trying to build your own relationships?"

"That doesn't matter, that's why we have each other," Brandi said walking back into the office. "We have always been there for each other, which is what makes our friendship so deep and great."

I'm gonna step out," Kendra said. She had been so damn quiet everyone forgot she was in the room. I'm gonna take the girls to get something to drink."

"No, Kendra stay, you are a part of us too," Dani said.

"Girl, sit you ass down," Vonne said.

"You mind as well get use to these types of conversations because they happen at any given moment," Nija said.

"Our niggas know how tight we are. They have no other choice but to respect it," Brandi said.

"The love I see in their eyes when they look at y'all is priceless. Now days you don't fine love like that," Kendra said. "That's a love worth fighting for."

"Kendra, the same love you're talkin' about I see it when Shyne looks at you," Nae said.

"I see it. I was just too afraid of being hurt again," Kendra said. "I feel the same way about him as he does me. I just don't wanna be let down."

"That's all a part of being in a relationship," Dani said. "Sometimes you will be let down as long as the love is still there," Dani said.

KNOCK! KNOCK!

Melo peeked his head inside. "Cherry, you have a few people who wants to talk to you," he said.

"Thanks," Cherry said as she made her way to the door.

"Ladies, I would love to continue this talk but I do have people here to see me," Cherry laughed.

Everyone followed her out her office.

*

The ladies walked out of Cherry's office laughing and joking to find the place still packed with people as music continued to play softly in the background.

"Let me kick it with you for a minute," Shyne said as she wrapped his arms around Kendra. She smiled.

"You finally have time for me?" She asked as they swayed back and forth to the beat.

"Ma, I will always have time for you," he said kissing her neck. "I just need for you to stop second guessing what we have."

"Can you fault a girl?" She asked. "Niggas play to many games and I can't afford for my heart to get hurt again."

"If you just trust and believe that the love I have for you is real. You would never have to worry about your heart getting broke again," Shyne said.

As if on cue, Brian McKnight You're The Only For Me, spilled from the speaker.

You say you've seen too many things,

that turn out to be too good to be true.

Against your better judgment, opened up your heart,

'til you found the joke was on you.

Looking out on the rest of our lives,

If we're gonna be together or apart

About the only way I know how to come,

is right straight from my heart.

I want you now,

I'll show you how

I can be the man you need me to be

I've been around,

But now I've found

That you're the only one for me.

Say you'll never fall again

You won't subject yourself to such pain

If you give me half a chance I will

Never leave you standing out in the rain

But if you think that I could look you in your face and lie right

Through my teeth

Then turn around and walk away

Cross my heart, girl I care for you

Shyne sung along in Kendra's ear. "Baby girl, you're the only one for me," he whispered in her ear.

"Shyne, if I didn't believe you didn't love me. I wouldn't be here," Kendra said as she turned to look into his eyes. "Just don't make me regret giving you a chance." She said kissing his lips.

*

Jacques was pissed that he had missed Anna. Jacques phone rung as he approached the door of Cherry's business. "Hello?" He answered as he continued looking around.

"Tell your girl this isn't over," Anna laughed. "Jacques, we could have been so happy together."

"Bitch, I don't want you. When will you get that thru that empty head of yours?" He asked. "You have crossed the line and when I get my hands on you it isn't gonna be pretty at all."

"We'll see about that," Anna said hanging up on Ques.

He was pissed but didn't wanna ruin Cherry's grand opening. He made his way back to store to continue support his woman. Jacques walked back inside to find the party still going. He spotted, Cherry talking to a few business people so he walked the other way, where his niggas were standing.

"We'll talk about this shit later. I don't wanna ruin my baby's night," Jacques said before any of his niggas could ask him what was going on.

For the rest of the night everyone enjoyed themselves and continued to support Cherry.

A few hours later it was just Cherry, Jacques, and their close friends.

"You did the damn thing," Dani said as Cherry took a seat.

"Thank you," Cherry smiled. "But I'm tired as hell." She said.

After holding a conversation for a while longer everyone began to help clean up the mess everyone else had left behind before they all went their separate ways.

Chapter Nineteen

Six Months Later.....

For the past six months life for Nae had been great. She was finally on the verge of opening her day care center like she had planned. Her and Kash relationship was getting back to how it used to be. Nae couldn't ask for more. She was happy and so were Kash, and their kids.

Nae was the first to wake up; she smiled as she looked over at a sleeping Kash. She kissed his forehead before she slid out of bed. She walked into the bathroom to take a shower. She woke up in a good mood. Nae turned the shower on as she hummed Hood Love by Mary.

She undressed and slipped her engagement ring off her finger before stepping into the shower. Nae turned on the radio in the shower. Future Ft Kelly Rowland Never End was playing. Nae sung along as she soaped her body.

A while later Nae was turning the shower off, grabbing her towel she wrapped it around her body before walking back into her room where she found Kash still sleep. Nae dried off before apply her favorite lotion to her skin. Nae threw on a tank top and a pair of sweats before she pulled her hair into a tight ponytail. She was gonna wake Kash but decided against it, all she was doing was running to the store for a few things so that she could cook breakfast. Before leaving she did leave him a little note to let him know where she was going just in case he indeed woke up before she returned. Nae checked on Keikeo and Lanaya before she left the house.

*

Maria had been gone for a while. She wanted for them to forget all about her, so that when she attracted they would be taken by surprised. But she was still underestimating Kash because he was indeed waiting on her to make a move. What he wasn't expected was for her move to be as deadly as it was gonna be.

"I told him I was gonna take someone very important from him just as he had done me." Maria thought as she looked in her rear-view mirror at the contents that sat on her back seat. She just hoped it was Nae who got stuck in her boobie trap and not Kash. Only, because she wanted him to suffer and feel her pain. She wanted him to know how it felt to lose someone that really mattered to you the most.

*

"Daddy, I'm hungry," Keikeo said as he jumped on the bed.

"Yeah, daddy, we hungry," Lanaya said as she jumped on the bed too.

Kash slowly opened his eyes to find his babies jumping all around his king size bed.

"Where is your mother?" He asked.

"We don't know," Keikeo said.

"Oh god, daddy, what is that smell?" Lanaya asked. Kash laughed as he got up to brush his teeth and wash his face.

"Daddy, did you brush your teeth last night?" Keikeo

asked.

"I don't think so. Because it smells bad," Lanaya said as the both of them continued jumping on the bed.

Kash walked into the bathroom and the first thing he spotted was Nae's engagement ring. He had asked her to never take it off again.

He washed his face and brushed his teeth before walking back into his room.

"Are you going to cook for us?" Keikeo asked, "Because I want pancakes."

"Me too, daddy, can we have pancakes with lots of syrup?" Lanaya asked.

"You two can have whatever y'all want," Kash said as he grabbed them both tickling them. Kash laughed as he watched them both squirm to get away.

"Let me call mommy to see where she is," Kash said as he stopped tickling them. He grabbed his cell dialing Nae's cell.

"What's up?" She answered on the second ring.

"So you went to the store without waking me up?" He asked sitting the note back on the nightstand.

"Yes, babe, I'm only goin' to the store to get a few things to cook us breakfast," Nae answered. "I didn't wanna wake you up because I was coming right back."

"Why aren't you wearing your engagement ring?" Kash asked.

"I'm sorry, I took it off to take a shower and rushed out forgetting to put it back on," Nae answered. "Papi, that won't happen again."

"A'ight, I love you, ma," Kash said.

"Mommy, I love you too," Keikeo said in the background.

"I love y'all too," Nae laughed. "I'll see you in a lil' while," Nae said hanging up.

"Daddy you love me too?" Lanaya asked hugging him.

"Yes, you know I love you, Keikeo, and mommy very much," answered Kash.

"No daddy I asked you if you loved me," Lanaya said. Kash laughed.

"Yes, I love you," he answered.

"Good, that means I can get a ring like mommy, right?" Kash continued to laugh as he picked them both up carrying them out of the room.

*

Cherry walked downstairs in search of her babies. A Saturday morning in her house was never quiet. Which only meant two things, One: Jacques had taken the kids with him or Two: they were doing something they had no business doing. Cherry could here JJ and Jewel laughing in the family room. Letting her know they were watching one of their favorite cartoons. "What are y'all...."

She stopped in mid-sentence when she found a woman's figure sitting in the middle of her sofa. While JJ sat on one side and Jewel on the other. Cherry could see the open bottle of Moscato and a wine glass sitting on her coffee table.

"I decided to keep them company until you decided to wake up," Anna said standing to her feet as she grabbed the wine glass before turning to face Cherry. Cherry frowned.

"JJ and Jewel come here now," Cherry said keeping her eyes on the Anna standing before her. Things had gone too far. She had involved her babies and that was a no-no.

"Why? We're watching TV. Come join us," she said wrapping her arms around Jewel and JJ.

"Yeah, mommy, come watch TV with us," Jewel said jumping up and down.

"JJ, grab your sister and go to your rooms," Cherry said balling her fist.

"Come on, Jewel," JJ said grabbing his sister's hand doing as Cherry had instructed him to do.

"Mommy, are we in trouble?" Jewel asked.

"No, just go to you room and don't come out until I tell you too," Cherry said.

Cherry watched as her babies ran up the stairs to their rooms before she turned her attention back to the bitch standing in the middle of her family room.

Cherry rushed into the room in attack mode. She quickly stopped in her tracks when she saw the gun pointed to her head.

"I wouldn't do that if I was you," she said sipping from her wine glass. "Didn't I tell you I didn't play well with others?"

"And didn't I tell you neither did I?" Cherry asked back.

"I have one big problem. You wanna know what that is?"

"What?" Cherry asked.

"You," she said pointing to Cherry. "Yo ass is in my way of happiness. You have everything I want and I can't have that."

"I see we are having some of the same issues," Cherry spat. "The only difference is I got who I want." Cherry said shrugging her shoulders.

"We've played this game long enough and it's time for it to be over," she said walking around the sofa. She paced around, Cherry holding the gun in one hand and the glass of wine in the other.

"This game has been over and you lost," Cherry said.

She laughed taking a drink from her glass as she stopped standing right in front of Cherry. "It ends today and so do your...."

Was all Anna got out as Cherry punched her in the face before grabbing for the gun. She dropped the glass as they fought for the gun. They both knew whoever ended up with the gun was the one who would survive that day. Cherry elbowed Anna in the face drawing blood from her nose but she never let go of the gun.

*

JJ grabbed his cell phone to call his father. Cherry and Ques had brought both him and Jewel a cell for purposes like these.

"Daddy, come home," JJ said into the phone when Jacques answered.

"What's the matter is everything okay?" Jacques asked.

"No, you have to get home, now," JJ said into the phone. Jacques could tell that something was wrong.

"I'm on my way now," Jacques said hanging up.

*

Jacques was getting a haircut. He had planned a special day for him and Cherry. It had been a while since just the two of them had done anything together. He paid for his cut rushing out the door. JJ had never called and told him he had to get home now. He dialed Cherry's phone hoping she could explain what was going on. When he didn't get an answer he dialed her number again. Getting her voicemail he jumped into his ride starting it up he eased into traffic.

The entire ride home Jacques kept calling Cherry's phone. He had no luck reaching her making him very nervous.

Jacques pulled up to his house in no time to find police cars pulling up as well.

"What the fuck goin' on?" He wondered stepping out the car.

"What's goin' on?" He asked the first officer to step out of the patrol car.

"Sir, we got a call from a little boy saying his mother needed help," the officer said.

POW! POW!

They heard two gun shots go off. The officers ducked as they drew their weapons. Jacques looked at them before running to his front door.

"And y'all mothafuckas supposed to protect and serve. But y'all scared of a few gun shots." He said over his shoulders.

"Sir you can't go in there!" A few officers yelled after him.

"Fuck y'all pig ass niggas. Who gonna stop me?" Jacques asked rushing into his home.

*

Nae entered the highway in her own zone. She switched lanes and picked up speed as she continued to rock out to Rihanna's CD.

Nae didn't bother looking at the caller ID because she thought it was Kash calling her again.

"Hello?" She answered.

"Bitch, I hope you're ready to die," Maria said into the phone. Nae removed the phone from her ear as she looked at the screen. She wanted to make sure she was hearing right. She knew she was. She could never forget Maria's voice.

"You may not know this, but Kash took someone very important from me and I'm repaying him for it. I warned him that I was gonna do this. He just didn't believe me," laughed Maria.

"I should have killed you when I had the chance," Nae spat.

"You should have but you didn't," Maria said. "And that was a big mistake on your part."

"Fuck you!" Nae spat.

"No, but I will make sure Kash fucks me every night. Nae, tell my father he can now rest in peace," Maria said. "Oh who am I kidding? Your ass is goin' straight to hell."

"Then I'm sure I can deliver the message to your sorry ass father," Nae assured.

"Thanks, and I'll be sure to mend Kash broken heart after he finds out you died in a bad car crash," laughed Maria.

"Oh look, it's gonna be Maria to the rescue."

"Maria, even when I'm gone I will still own his heart. Good luck trying to get what will always belong to me," Nae said hanging up on her.

Nae was doing 95 MPH, she stepped on the break and nothing happened. Her car was still going 95 miles and there was nothing she could do about it. Nae looked in her rear-view mirror as tears cascaded down her face. She thanked god that her babies wasn't in the car with her. Nae knew she was dying. She now wondered if she could have prevented all of the bullshit in the first place.

Nae smiled as she thought about all the good times her and Kash shared. Even all the arguments they had. Some were small ones, ones that they could have just walked away and others had proven just how strong their love for each other was. They had weathered one storm of Gangsta Luv. Their storm was ending right there on that highway.

*

Jacques rushed into the family room to find Cherry and another body laid face down as blood quickly spilled from either one or both their bodies.

"Noooo!" Jacques screamed as he grabbed at his dreads. "CHERRY! Please, baby answer me," he said as he walked over to view the damage that was done.

"Sir..."

"Shut the fuck up!" Jacques barked as he checked on Cherry. He knew Anna was gone because he was looking into her dead eyes.

Cherry slowly eased from the floor. Jacques helped her up as he hugged her tightly.

"Jacques, get the fuck off me!" Cherry yelled. "My fuckin' babies are here!" Cherry yelled pushing him. Cherry walked over and stood over Anna's dead body. "Bitch, I told you fuckin' with me wasn't something you wanted to do. You played your game and lost," Cherry said as she spit or Anna's dead body.

"Ma'am, can you tell us what happened?" One of the officers asked.

"Figure that shit out," Cherry said as she stormed out the room to check on her kids.

She rushed up the stairs and into their room.

"Are you okay, mommy?" JJ asked.

"Mommy, did you kick her butt again?" Jewel asked unaware of how serious the problem was.

Cherry didn't breathe a word as she hugged both JJ and Jewel tight.

"Are you two okay?" Cherry asked checking just to make sure no harm was done to either of them.

"We are fine," Jewel answered.

"Why are you crying?" JJ asked as he wiped the tears

away. Cherry looked into her babies' faces and broke down again. There was no way in hell she could explain to a three and four year old what had taken place downstairs.

*

Kash wanted to know what was taking Nae so long to return from the store if she was only going to pick up a few things.

"Daddy, do we have to wait for mommy?" Keikeo asked, "Because I'm hungry, now."

"I'm gonna make y'all some pancakes," Kash said getting up from his seat.

"Daddy, I hope you make them like mommy do," Lanaya said never turning away from the kitchen.

Kash checked the time and saw that Nae had been gone for over an hour. "*It doesn't take that long to run to the store.*" He thought reaching for his cell inside his pocket. Before Kash had any time to do anything it rung.

He didn't recognize the number but he answered anyways.

"Who is this?" He answered.

"Kash," Maria said. Kash could tell she was laughing about something.

"Why are you callin' me?" He asked moving around the kitchen.

"Remember when I said that I was gonna take something that meant the world to you because you did it to me?" She asked. "Well, be keeping an eye on the news. They will be bearing bad news for someone," she laughed before disconnecting the call.

Kash stomach knotted up. He didn't like the sound of that. He just prayed it was all a bad dream or a bad joke. He quickly dialed Nae's number. "Baby, please pick up," he mumbled over and over again. "Nae, pick up the fuckin' phone!" Kash said dialing her number again. Please don't do this to me," Kash begged. He sighed deeply as he rushed into the living room to check the news.

"Hey, daddy, we were watching that," Lanaya said looking up at Kash.

"I know and I'm sorry, I need to watch the news," he said as he flipped to the news channel.

Hi, I'm David Barns reporting to you live on Interstate 580 where just under thirty minutes ago there was a terrible car accident involving an eighteen wheeler and several cars. Police are still on the scene trying to piece together what caused the accident. As of now the police have confirmed three people have died and four are facing life threaten injuries. As of now the police aren't releasing the names of the victims or the injured.

I'm David Barns, reporting to you live. Back to you guys in the studio.

Kash felt sick to his stomach. He dropped to his knees, praying that Nae wasn't any of the people hurt or worst dead.

"Are you okay?" Lanaya asked walking over to Kash. "Why are you crying?" She asked.

Kash grabbed her as he waved Keikeo over. He took both of them into his arms squeezing them tightly. Kash released his kids and looked them into their eyes.

He saw nothing but innocents. He knew when they got older it would change to hate and resentment. "Come on," he said picking them both up.

"Are we going to get something to eat?" Lanaya asked, "Because I'm hungry."

"Auntie Kendra will make y'all all the pancakes y'all want. Daddy has to make a quick run," Kash said rushing out the door. He helped them into their car seats before he walked around getting into the driver's seat.

*

Kendra was in the kitchen making herself and Shyne a nice breakfast when someone began banging on her front door. She dried her hands on a dish towel before making her way to the front door.

"Ma, I got it," Shyne said as he stopped her. "Are you expecting anyone?" He asked.

"No, but you know it's nothing for Nae ass to just pop up unannounced," laughed Kendra.

Shyne opened the door to find Kash standing there with Lanaya and Keikeo standing by his side. He didn't have to breathe a word for Shyne to know that something was wrong.

"What's good?" Shyne asked. Kash ignored him as he searched for Kendra.

"Ken, I know this is short notice but I need for you to hold my babies down for a while," Kash said. He was trying to hold back the tears but a few slid down his cheek.

"Is everything okay?" She asked.

"No, auntie we hungry," Lanaya said with her hands on her hips.

"I can't explain it now but I swear when I get back I will," Kash said walking to the door.

"Hold up, bruh," Shyne said as he grabbed his shirt. "Babe, I'll be back." He said kissing Kendra on the lips.

Kendra looked down at Keikeo and Lanaya. "It's just us three," Kendra said as she turned to walk into the kitchen. "What do you guys wanna eat?" She asked.

"Pancakes," they sung. Kendra laughed.

"I should have known."

*

Shyne sat quietly in the passenger seat while Kash drove. The first ten minutes of the ride was a quiet one. He was hoping Kash would have said what was bothering him but he never did. "Are you ever gonna let me in on what's goin' on?" Shyne asked.

"Nae's dead," Kash said as he kept his eyes on the road.

"What?" Shyne asked. "I mean how did that happen?"

"That bitch Maria," Kash said as he headed for the highway. He knew there was no way he would be able to enter onto it. He would leave his car running and walk on the sense. "She did something to Nae's fuckin' car," Kash said as tears rolled down his face.

"Sir, you cannot go over there," an officer said stopping Kash with a firm hand to his chest.

"Fuck you mean I can't go over there? My lady was in one of those mothafuckin' cars," Kash said slapping the officer's hand away.

"Sir, the only thing I can tell you is to head to the hospital," the officer said stopping Kash once again. Kash nostrils flared. "The sight isn't pretty." He finished.

"Is there anything you can tell me?" Kash asked already knowing the answer to his question.

"I'm afraid I can't do that," the officer said. Kash took a deep breath as he balled his fist.

"Bruh, let's go," Shyne said before Kash decided to do anything stupid.

"Nah, fuck that. I know these mothafuckas can tell me something," Kash spat.

"Kash, you can't afford to get locked up. Don't give these pig ass niggas a reason to," Shyne said pulling Kash away from the officer.

Kash walked away without any problems, his heart ached. He wasn't sure if Nae was really dead and gone but from the looks and sounds of things she was. And he blamed himself. If he would have never fucked with Maria, none of this would be happening right now. Nae would still be alive; guilt is something he would live with for the rest of his life.

*

Later on that night, Kash was still waiting to hear any type of News about Nae but nothing.

"Hello?" He answered his ringing phone.

"Didn't I tell you I was goin' to have the last laugh?" Maria asked as she laughed.

"Bitch, when I catch you, I swear I'm gonna kill you," Kash gritted into the phone.

Maria laughed. "Kamil, by the time you think about lookin' for me, I'm goin' to be long gone," she assured.

"That's your best bet," Kash spat.

"I told you I was gonna take someone that meant the world to you as you did to me. I just don't understand what she had that I didn't?" Maria said.

"My heart, she was everything you weren't and can't another bitch ever change that," Kash answered.

"I've learned that but at least you will be miserable with me," Maria said.

"I can never be miserable when I have my kids," Kash said.

"Well, Kash, it was nice talkin' to you. Don't work too hard lookin' for me," Maria laughed as she disconnected the call.

Before Kash could put his phone back in his pocket his phone rang again.

"Hello?" He answered. Kash listened to the Detective

inform him of who his was and why he was calling. Kash held his breath as he listened to him talk.

When he hung up the phone the tears were falling from his eyes at a rapid pace. The Detective had just informed him that Nae's car was indeed one of the many involved in the car crash that happened hours prior. The only thing they couldn't confirm was a body.

"How am I gonna break the bad news to her girls, let alone our kids?" Kash asked himself.

Epilogue

Three Months Later.....

Kash sat in the front row of the funeral home crying while he held Lanaya in one hand and Keikeo in the other. A lot of people had come out to show their last respect and to say their final goodbye to Nae. Kash still didn't believe it but the proof was lying right in front of his eyes in a purple casket trimmed in white diamonds. That's right; he had to send his baby home in style. There wasn't a day that went by that he didn't miss her or wish he could switch places with her.

He sat there listening to the pastor talk about Nae, and how her life had been cut short. It was starting to become too much but he knew this was only the beginning of what he had to deal with. When the pastor was done speaking everyone began to move around Kash. He was stuck, he wanted someone to wake him from the terrible dream he was having. Kash knew it wasn't a dream. He knew this is what he reality had come too.

"Daddy, mommy looks so pretty in that picture," Lanaya said tapping Kash on the arm bringing him from his thoughts.

"Daddy, where is mommy? Everybody is here to see her," Keikeo said causing Kash to break down. How was he gonna tell his three year old twins that their mother was dead and never coming back?

"If it isn't Mr. Swing ding-a-ling," Vonne said now standing in front of Kash.

"Vonne, fall the fuck back. I'm not in the mood," Kash warned.

"Nigga, I don't give a fuck what you're not in the mood for. You foul," she spat letting him know just how she felt. "You should be lying in the bitch, not her. And because of ya fucked up ways she isn't here to see her kids grow," Vonne said.

Kash sat Keikeo and Lanaya down before standing up. By now all eyes were on them.

"Vonne, chill the fuck out," Jason said grabbing her arm. She yanked from his grip.

"I'm not chillin' anything."

"You don't think I feel bad about this?" Kash asked. "If I could I'll trade places with her in a heartbeat!" Kash yelled. "I just lost the love of my fuckin' life. I can't hold her any more, nor can I hear her voice ever again. I can't hold her and tell her I love her. I can't do any of that shit no more. My kids are motherless and how the fuck am I gonna tell them their mother is dead and never coming back?" He asked with tears running down his face at a rapid pace. "None of you mothafuckas know what I'm goin' thru so miss me with that bullshit," he said turning around to pick his twins up.

Vonne and everyone else standing or sitting in the overcrowded funeral home watched as Kash grabbed his babies and stormed out.

"Bye," Vonne said as she waved him bye.

"Vonne, you were cold for that," Ray said.

"How, when I was only speaking the truth," she said turning to rub the top of the closed casket. "Damn, my bitch really gone," she said holding her tears back.

"Y'all know this is not how Nae wanted to go out. This sad shit isn't her at all," Dani said.

"Word, Nae loved getting her party on," Nija said.

Cherry was the only one who was yet to speak. Everyone knew she had taken Nae's death the hardest. They were all close but Cherry and Nae was the closest of the crew.

"Please somebody wake me from this nightmare," Cherry said crying. She had been tryna be strong but seeing the casket and Nae's picture sitting on top, she couldn't hold back anymore.

"I wish this was a bad dream," Brandi said.

"How could this happen? I mean why?" Cherry asked wiping the tears away. The more she wiped the more tears fell from her eyes.

"I'll be back," Vonne said walking off.

"Where are you goin'? Ray asked.

Vonne ignored her as she continued to walk off.

"How could Kash let things get this bad?" Ray asked.

"Fuck Kash!" Cherry spat. She wasn't feeling him to tough right about now and she wasn't sure if she would ever speak to him again. "This is his entire fault."

"Can I have everyone's attention?" Vonne said into the mic. "For all you who knew Nae knew she wasn't for this sad shit. She was always the life of the party. She was always somewhere ready to shake her ass," laughed Vonne. "And I'm sure she wants us all to remember her that way. So dry ya eyes and let's get it poppin'. She said about to walk off. "Oh and before I forget, all you lurking ass hoes fall back because Kash is still of the market, good day." She said finally walking off.

*

Hours later Kash finally walked thru his front door holding his babies in his arms. Everyone got quiet as they looked at him. He looked like shit, and they knew he had been crying his eyes out. He put Keikeo and Lanaya down and they ran off in search of Jewel and JJ. Kash knew her girls were feeling some type of way about him right now. He also knew he would be hearing just how they felt.

Kash looked up to find all eyes on him. He saw hurt, sadness, worry, and pain sitting on all of Nae's girl's faces. He knew none of them were feeling him to tough but at this point he didn't give a fuck. He was without the love of his life while they stood around with their better half.

"Kash!" Cherry called out. "This is all ya fuckin' fault!" She yelled as she charged at him. Kash never moved as Cherry rained blows all over his face and chest. "She isn't supposed to be dead," Cherry cried.

Jacques grabbed Cherry but she yanked from his grip.

"It should have been you we were lowering into the ground and not Nae," Cherry spat.

Kash had heard enough.

"Hold the fuck up," he said getting everyone's attention. "If I could, I would trade places with Nae without a doubt in my mothafuckin' mind. And yes I take most of the blame for what has happened and that's something I have to live with for the rest of my mothafuckin' life. But you, none of you will keep disrespecting me. At the end of today and any other day after this you all are goin' home to the one you love. Not me. None of you mothafuckas have to explain to your kids that their mother is never coming back," Kash spat. "I loved and still do love Nae to pieces. That will never change," he said removing his button up shirt. He turned to show the tattoo of Nae of his back, "She told me to get her name tatted on me so that she knew it was real. I got her whole mothafuckin' body tatted." He said turning to face them one again.

"Kash, where is, Maria?" Ray asked.

"If I had the answer to that the bitch would have been dead already," he said. "But y'all better believe when I do find that bitch, she's gonna wish like hell she never met me," he assured before walking off. Kash stopped in his tracks turning to face his niggas and their ladies.

"I don't know why I just stood there explaining anything to any of you. The only person I had to explain anything to is fuckin' dead. Get the fuck out!" Kash spat pointing to the door.

"Did that nigga just put us out?" Vonne asked.

"I'm gonna let that slide, only because I know my nigga hurting right now," Brandi said.

"Come on y'all cut him some slack," Nija said. "He just lost his wife." They weren't married on paper but that didn't matter.

"He's right. None of us knows what he's goin' thru," Dani said. "We are supposed to hold him down not push him away."

"Pointing the finger isn't gonna change shit," Ray said.

"Seriously?" Cherry asked with her hands on her hips. "You mothafuckin' right I'm pointing the finger and placing the blame on, Kash," she said. "If he would have never fucked that so called crazy bitch or brought her a house, or paid for her plastic skin, none of this would have gone down."

"You can't say that," Rell spoke.

"Word, none of us knows what would have happened," Melo said.

"We can sit here pointing the finger and placing the blame all day until we turn blue in the face, that isn't gonna change anything," Chase said.

"What we need to be doin' is finding that bitch, Maria," King said.

"That's something I can agree on," Ray said. She had wanted to kill Maria for a while now.

*

Kash paced his room floor with tears running down his face. Today was the first day of many that he would be living without his love, Nae. Kash laid across his bed placing his arms behind his head as he thought about all the things he could have done differently.

Now he would live the rest of his days with regret, hurt, and, pain. No one understood how he felt or what he was going through. Like he had said before, he was the one who would have to live the rest of his life, blaming himself or without the woman he had planned on marrying one day. He would never get to do any of the things he had promised Nae.

"Baby, I fuckin' miss you already," Kash mumbled as he wiped the tears from his eyes, but the tears wouldn't stop falling. "I promise you I'm goin' to find that bitch and do her dirty."

Kash reached into his pocket pulling out Nae's engagement ring. He brought it to his lips and kissed the diamond.

The End